DIVIDED LOYALTIES

David J. Jones

ARTHUR H. STOCKWELL LTD
Torrs Park   Ilfracombe   Devon
Established 1898
www.ahstockwell.co.uk

© David J. Jones, 2011
First published in Great Britain, 2011
All rights reserved.
No part of this publication may be reproduced
or transmitted in any form or by any means,
electronic or mechanical, including photocopy,
recording, or any information storage and
retrieval system, without permission
in writing from the copyright holder.

British Library Cataloguing-in-Publication Data.
A catalogue record for this book is available
from the British Library.

This is a work of fiction. Names, characters, places and incidents are
the product of the author's imagination and any resemblance to actual
persons, living or dead, events or locales, is purely coincidental.

ISBN 978-0-7223-4092-9
*Printed in Great Britain by
Arthur H. Stockwell Ltd
Torrs Park   Ilfracombe
Devon*

DAVID J. JONES – BIOGRAPHICAL DETAILS

I started writing poetry as a hobby in 1992, before writing the first draft of *Divided Loyalties* in 1997. In 1998, I began to have some poems chosen for anthologies through Forward Press, Cambridgeshire, and developed an interest in self-publishing my work.

Since 2000, I have published my own poetry books as a self-publishing poet. These include:

Little Book of Poems – through Forward Press.
Faith into Words – through ProPrint.
The Sun Shines Through – through ProPrint.
From Me To You – desktop publication.
Simple Truths – desktop publication.
Not in Our Own Strength – desktop publication.
Personal Experiences – desktop publication.
Personal Reflections – desktop publication.
Personal Favourites – desktop publication.

I am a Christian, and all my writing is a reflection of my experience of faith. *Divided Loyalties* is my first novel.

CHAPTER ONE

Almost as soon as the telephone call was made, the police sirens could be heard across the housing estate. Running for their lives, each of the boys involved in the trouble headed for home – all except one.

Not for the first time, the feelings of fear and regret regarding what the Gang had done brought him into a panic-stricken moment. He didn't know what to do. As the sirens drew closer, he opened the door to a block of flats, frantically climbed the first two flights of stairs to a landing, and observed the activities taking place in the street from a window that overlooked the road.

Some of his friends were still running home along the main road, as if relishing the danger of being caught by the police. One or two had made it home, as they lived nearby. Others were running along the footpath next to the brook that ran through the middle of the estate.

He suddenly realised that he was the only one left near the scene of the crime. He watched as two police cars and an ambulance pulled up a few yards along the road.

The officers from the first car went to the scene of the crime, then told the other officers to search for the boys. The officers from the second car began to cross the field behind the flats, looking intently for the culprits. They returned a few minutes later, having failed to locate any of them, and drove away to patrol the estate.

As the car disappeared out of sight, he gave a sigh of relief and began to calm down.

Just then, he heard the door to the block of flats slam loudly beneath him. He heard footsteps approaching him at a hurried pace. An ice-cold chill ran down his spine!

Expecting the worst, he turned to surrender, only to sigh with relief again. It was a man who lived on the top floor of the block, late home from work. He passed by so quickly that he hardly noticed the adolescent on the stairway, gazing at him.

As the stranger closed the door to his flat, the young teenager gathered his thoughts and began to think what he would do next. He stood there for a few moments, finishing a canned drink for refreshment. He wondered if the police car would return, or if it had left the estate. He glanced out of the window and saw that several people were standing on the embankment outside the flats where the incident had occurred. To get home, he would have to cross the field behind the flats, get to the brook, and then make his way to the shopping centre before crossing the main road and entering the street where he lived. His friends were long gone by now, and he could catch up with them again in the morning at school.

Karl Edwards had never wanted to be a part of a gang that caused so much trouble. All he wanted to do was hang out with his mates and have a good time. Deep down, he was a good lad, but he had got in with the wrong crowd. He knew this truth, but couldn't see a way out of his circumstances. His best friends were part of the Gang because the gang leader had bullied them into joining. Karl had started to hang out with the Gang because of them: he wanted to make sure they didn't get into any trouble. Yet here he was facing a situation where he could be caught for a crime he didn't commit.

Throwing his empty can on the grass, he began to run home as quickly as possible. It would not take him long if he ran all the way, but he would take no chances. He checked all around as he approached his house, to see if anyone was following him.

As he closed the garden gate, he saw a police car enter the street. Karl hid behind his dad's shed and braced himself for trouble. The officers could not see him from the patrol car. As the car passed, Karl fumbled for his key, found it, and made for the front door.

He closed the front door behind him and ran upstairs to his bedroom. Throwing his jacket to the floor, he took off his T-shirt, which was soaked through with sweat, entered the bathroom and washed himself down. He put on a new T-shirt and flopped on to his bed.

Turning his head, he checked the time. His mum would be home soon from her second cleaning job of the day. Karl had to make sure she didn't suspect anything. He put a CD on, then began playing some computer games.

Within half an hour, his mum was home. They spoke briefly, then she went to watch television. Karl stayed in his room and continued playing his games. He eventually fell asleep two hours later, unaware of his drunken father finally coming home from the pub just after midnight.

CHAPTER TWO

Ever since he had joined the Gang, Karl had dreaded going to school. He didn't like Jed and Cooper, the gang leaders; they had been bullies ever since primary school. He was only in the Gang because they had forced his friends, Richie, Tommy and Andrew to follow them.

As he walked to school that morning, Karl remembered the first night he had hung out with the group. His mum and dad had been having a serious row and his mum suggested he go out for a while until things calmed down.

As Karl had approached the small shopping centre in the middle of the estate, he had seen his three friends. When he met them, Jed had walked over and asked Karl if he could lend him some money, which Karl did. From that moment, Jed and Cooper had been very friendly and, for a while, Karl had got on with them.

That was before the trouble started.

Jed and Cooper started to push the boys into doing things that were dangerous and sometimes criminal. They threatened the boys with violence if they didn't do as they said, ruling over them through fear. Karl didn't like it at all!

To keep the peace, and to protect himself and his friends, Karl went along with what Jed and Cooper told him to do. This resulted in his getting into trouble on the estate and in school, as well as seeing a decline in his school work, which had been of a good standard.

Most of his teachers had spoken to his form tutor, Mrs Phillips, about their concerns; she too had seen a change in Karl's attitude in class.

Karl was very unhappy. He didn't want to be a part of a gang that caused so much trouble. Perhaps that was why he had been walking so far behind them when Jed had thrown the brick through the old lady's window. Karl had called into the petrol station to buy a drink, and he had made no effort to catch up with the boys as they walked up the hill ahead of him. He had enjoyed those few moments alone.

Karl knew he had to leave the Gang if he was going to be happy again. His problem was knowing how to. He needed to find an alternative way to live his life – a way that would keep him from any trouble the Gang was getting into.

As he entered the school grounds, he knew his mum and dad couldn't help him. Things had become very difficult between his parents ever since his dad had lost his job. His mum had taken on a second cleaning job to keep up the income of the household, and her work now kept her away from home every morning and evening. Karl only saw her at breakfast time, and late in the evening when she arrived home. She had already left for work when he arrived home from school.

Karl didn't see much of his dad either. During the day, he was out either looking for work, or at a mate's house, or in the betting shop, wasting his mum's hard-earned money. He spent the evenings in the pub, and only came home when the landlord threw him out at closing time. Karl spent most of his time at home on his own. This was another reason Karl was with the Gang: he liked company and did not enjoy being in the house alone.

Karl saw no answer to his predicament, and he prepared himself for another difficult day with the boys.

Looking up, he saw Tommy and Andrew walking ahead of

him. As he quickened his pace to catch them up, he felt a hand grab him from behind and pull him on to the school field.

"Edwards! Where were you last night?"

It was Jed.

"I—"

Karl was stopped from explaining.

"You'd better come and see me at break time, or you're in for it!"

Jed ran off, clipped one of the girls from their class on the back of the head, and made his way to meet up with Cooper.

"I can't wait!" said Karl sarcastically as he watched the villainous figure disappear.

CHAPTER THREE

Karl's favourite sport was football; his favourite team was Liverpool. Whenever he played football, he imagined he was playing for them.

The games changing room was never a pleasant place to be, and his crowd were the last people Karl wanted to be with. As the class lined up to go into the changing room, Karl wondered what prank would be pulled this week. Usually Jed or Cooper had something planned for one of the boys, whether they were in the Gang or not. That morning, though, there wasn't time for any nonsense. One of the games teachers stayed in the changing room while the other checked the sports equipment. Some of the parents had complained about the trouble being caused by Jed and Cooper, and the teacher was making sure nothing happened before the lesson started.

The Gang was split up in games, as the teachers usually picked the teams. Karl was relieved not to be put in a team with either Jed or Cooper, but he was glad when Richie was chosen to be on his side.

The game passed quickly. Karl scored a couple of goals in his side's victory. He felt good as he chatted to his teammates on the way back to the changing room. Just as everything seemed to be going well, the teachers were called out to assist with something in the hall, which was next to the changing room. Then it happened!

One boy in the group was a regular to be picked on. Jed jumped on top of him, pushing him to the floor. Cooper then kicked him in the stomach.

The other boys stood back in fear, scared to get involved in case they got the rough treatment too. Karl had seen it all before, and far too often.

As the bell went for break, and the two bullies left the room, Karl went up to the victim and helped him to his feet. Paul wasn't one of Karl's favourite boys in the class. Physically he was small and weak – an academic, who did well in school most of the time. Karl knew this was why Jed always picked on him. Even so, Karl was sick of seeing Paul being treated so badly.

"Are you all right?" asked Karl.

The boy nodded, sobbing slightly because of the pain he was in. "I'm OK, thanks," he replied, taking his school bag from his friend David.

Karl felt guilty.

"I'm sorry I didn't stop them. I didn't think they would do anything this week."

"That's OK, Karl – it's not your fault."

As they left the changing room, Paul hesitantly turned to Karl.

"Is it . . . ?"

"Is it what?" asked Karl.

"Well, you know them. I mean, you're one of them."

Paul's words hurt Karl deeply as they continued to talk.

"Why do they do it? Is it because I'm small or something?"

"I think so." Karl shrugged his shoulders as if to show he didn't know the real answer.

"Is it because I'm in the school orchestra?"

"Possibly."

"Or because I do well in school?"

"Maybe." Karl was getting bored of Paul's questions.

"Or is it because I go to church?"

Paul's question completely threw Karl.

"What! You go to church?"

"Yes, we both do," said Paul, turning to David.

"Why?" asked Karl.

"Well, I started going when I was very young," admitted Paul. "My parents are Christians. They took me to Sunday school."

"And I started going last year, when I joined the youth club," David added.

"Youth club?" asked Karl.

"Yeah, we meet every Friday and Saturday. We do lots of things," David replied. "We've even got a football team. We play six-a-side against other churches in a league. We won the cup last year. The church gave us a treat for doing so."

"What was that – a new hymn book each?" Karl asked sarcastically.

David grinned. "Not exactly, Karl. We went to Anfield to see Liverpool play a league match."

"What!" Karl gasped.

Paul explained: "Our minister, Mike, is a big Liverpool fan. He used to live there. He promised us a trip to see Liverpool play if we won something last season, and – well, he came through."

Karl couldn't believe what he was hearing. A church group going to Anfield? He had gone to Sunday school several years before, and had been totally disinterested in it. Nothing like that had even been mentioned when he had attended the local church.

Karl continued to talk to Paul and David during the break. What they had told him so far had caught his attention.

"But isn't church boring?" asked Karl.

"No," replied Paul. "Our church is very modern. We have all sorts of things going on especially for the youth."

"Listen, Karl: you're good at football," said David. "Why don't you come along on Friday and maybe we can get you into the team. You'd have to see Mike first before—"

David was suddenly interrupted.

"Hey, Edwards, where you bin? Come on! Jed wants a word with you."

One of the boys from the Gang had returned to find Karl, and he cut in on David's words.

"Sorry," said Karl to David. "I've got to go."

Without hesitation, Karl left with his friend to join the Gang, leaving Paul and David feeling bewildered.

CHAPTER FOUR

There was no time to meet with Jed. As soon as Karl walked away to find him, the bell went for the next lesson. Karl and Jed were in different classes for the rest of the morning. Their meeting would have to wait until lunchtime.

As Karl arrived at the dinner queue, he was met by Jed's stern face. Cooper looked at his best mate, then at Karl, wondering if the stare was causing fear inside him. Karl was too hungry to care. Besides, he had seen it all before. Jed always stared in the same way when he was angry, which was pretty much all the time.

Half an hour later, they were sitting in their usual spot on the school grounds. Cooper was striking matches against the concrete wall, while Jed paced back and forth as if agitated by something. He then turned to face the Gang.

"Right, you lot, listen and listen good! I heard from one o' my teachers that the fuzz are at the school to do with last night. If any of you give me and Cooper away, you'll be on the receiving end o' this!"

Jed reached into one of the pockets of his jacket and pulled out a large flick knife. None of the boys, except Cooper, had known that he was carrying it.

"Hey, don' – don't you worry, Jed!" said Andrew nervously. "We didn't see a thing – right, guys?"

The other lads nodded in agreement, as they fearfully looked at Jed's weapon.

"You'd better not 'ave! Anyone gives me away, and I'll kill yer! Now scram! We'll meet tonight – usual place."

Karl turned to leave with Richie, but Cooper stopped him.

"Not you, Edwards," said Jed coldly. "We need to 'ave a little chat!"

The other boys stopped and looked back, wondering what was going to happen.

"I told you lot t' beat it! Now get outa here!" ordered Jed.

"Go on – get lost!" Cooper shouted menacingly.

The boys hurried away, fearing the outcome if they stayed. Tommy, Andrew and Richie waited for Karl out of Jed and Cooper's sight, concerned about their friend and what they would do to him.

Jed walked up to Karl. The sun glinted off the knife's blade into Karl's eyes as Jed waved it threateningly in front of him.

"Well now, Edwards, what am I gonna do with you?"

Karl didn't flinch. He stood calmly, controlling the fear that was building inside him. He didn't want Jed to see that he was scared.

"Why weren't you walking with us last night?" asked Jed.

"I went to buy a drink – you know that," answered Karl.

"Yeah, took you a long time, though, didn't it?"

"The queue was long," replied Karl. "It was ages before I was served."

"That's a load of rubbish!"

Jed was not impressed by Karl's excuse. He looked intently at Karl, then nodded to Cooper. Cooper grabbed Karl by his shirt collar and pushed him up against the wall behind him.

"Now listen, Edwards, and listen well. If you're goin' to be in the Gang, you gotta do as you're told," ordered Cooper. "You understand?"

The tighter Cooper gripped him, the more Karl wanted to leave the Gang. For some reason, Paul and David entered his mind.

"You got it?" bellowed Jed.

The next thing Karl knew, he was lying on the ground, holding his stomach. Cooper thumped him hard, then kicked him when he had fallen down. Jed turned Karl over, held the knife to his throat, and pressed his face to Karl's.

"Next time, Edwards, you keep with us, right?"

"OK," replied Karl quietly.

Cooper kicked him again.

"What was that, Edwards? We didn't hear you!"

"OK, OK!" replied Karl loudly.

Jed put his knife away, pulled Karl up and threw him back against the wall.

"And if you 'ave anything more to do with them two geeks, you'll meet Cooper's fist again!"

"What, David and Paul? We were only talking," protested Karl.

"You have nothin' more to do with them! You speak to them again and I'll—"

Cooper suddenly interrupted Jed: "Jed, Mr Johnson's coming!"

Jed turned to Karl. "Not a word, Edwards, or else!"

Mr Johnson was about to pass by when he noticed the state Karl was in.

"What happened to you, son?" he asked.

"I—"

Karl didn't know what to say. One wrong word and he knew that Jed and Cooper would do something worse to him than they had already done.

"He tripped over his bag, sir," suggested Cooper.

Mr Johnson looked at Cooper's grinning face and suspected he was lying.

17

"Do you need any help, lad?"

"No, I'm . . ." Karl looked across at Jed and Cooper. "I'm OK, thanks, sir."

Mr Johnson continued his tour of the school and left Karl to sort himself out. Karl looked across at his two adversaries. They were grinning back at him, enjoying their moment of victory.

"I'll see you later, Edwards," said Jed threateningly. "Don't be late or you'll get worse than what you've just had!"

Jed and Cooper walked off, leaving Karl to sort himself out alone.

CHAPTER FIVE

Half an hour into the afternoon's lessons, a hastily arranged assembly was called in the hall for the whole of Karl's school year. Some pupils were hoping for lessons to be cancelled so they could go home and enjoy an afternoon off; others wondered at the mystery behind the gathering.

Karl was still aching after his confrontation with Jed and Cooper. As he took his seat in the hall, he saw Paul and David sitting a few rows in front of him. His mind went back to their conversation that morning.

A moment later, the assembly stood as the headmaster walked in, closely followed by Police Sergeant Haynes. The Sergeant was a tall, rugged man, and, through his years of service in the police force, he had dealt with many different situations involving young people. This was not the first time he had found himself addressing a school assembly. The headmaster introduced Sergeant Haynes, who then took over and spoke to the pupils.

"Last night, an elderly lady on the estate was the victim of a violent attack. Someone threw a brick through her window, causing her multiple injuries as well as considerable damage to her property."

Jed and Cooper grinned at each other. Paul immediately began to pray silently for the old lady. Karl started to feel uneasy as a haunting silence fell over the room. The Sergeant continued:

"From the witnesses we interviewed last night, we have

gathered enough information to lead us to believe that a group of boys from this school was near the flat at the time of the incident. We think that one of them is responsible for what happened. We have spent the morning interviewing lads from other school years. Now, this afternoon, we will be conducting interviews for this school year."

Some of the other boys from the Gang sniggered aloud. The Sergeant focused his attention on them.

"And in case any of you think you'll avoid being investigated," he said in a raised voice, "we have the names and addresses of all the boys we want to talk to. If anyone avoids coming to the interviews, we will be visiting them at home. In the meantime, if anyone has information regarding the incident last night, or knows anyone who does, I want you to come and see me as soon as possible, or tell one of your teachers. This criminal must be brought to justice, and the sooner the better!"

Sergeant Haynes read out the names of the first boys he wanted to speak to, then left the assembly with them to begin the interviews. The headmaster dismissed the pupils, and they got up to leave, row by row. Karl turned around and, glancing to the other side of the hall, he saw one of the girls from his class crying. It was Kayleigh – a girl who lived a few doors away from him. As they left the hall, he managed to catch up with her.

"Kayleigh, what's wrong?" he asked concernedly.

Kayleigh's friend Debbie had an arm around her, comforting Kayleigh.

"It was her great-nan who was hurt in the incident last night, Karl," explained Debbie. "Whoever did this put her in hospital. She was very badly injured. The thug! If I get my 'ands on 'im, I'll do 'im over!"

Debbie, as Karl knew, was not a girl to be messed with!

As Debbie continued telling Karl about Kayleigh's

great-grandmother, a horror fell over him. He knew Kayleigh very well. Her family had moved into the street at the time Kayleigh and Karl had started primary school. She had been a good friend to him ever since. He had met her great-grandmother several times over the years, when she had visited Kayleigh's family.

As the girls walked away to their next lesson, Karl stood in shock. He was part of a group of boys who had hurt someone dear to someone he knew so well. How could he stand by and let Jed get away with it? What should he say to the police when they interviewed him?

Before he could decide, Jed found him.

"Well now, Edwards, what's wrong with you, talking to the girls! Got a crush on one of them, eh?"

Cooper laughed.

"It was Kayleigh's great-nan who was hurt last night," said Karl toughly.

"So?" Jed's voice was empty of concern.

"Well, it's just—"

Jed put his hand over Karl's mouth.

"When you get called in by the fuzz, you don't say a word – or else!"

Jed opened his jacket so that Karl could see the handle of his flick knife in the inner pocket.

"You get the message, Edwards?"

Karl sighed and nodded his head. "Yeah, I get the message, Jed."

"Good. Now, me and Cooper are going home – bad stomach and all that. You say a word and—"

"I get the message," said Karl.

"Good! I'll see you later, Edwards!"

Jed and Cooper ran off, leaving Karl to make his way to his next class.

Karl couldn't settle into the lesson. His name was near the top of the register – he knew he could be called soon. The boys whose names had been called out in the hall returned to the class, and another couple of boys were called out to be interviewed by the police. Karl became more and more tense, but, like everything else, he kept it inside. No one could see his anxiety.

The bell rang for the end of the school day. Karl had not been called. He gathered his stuff together and headed for home as quickly as possible, not waiting for his friends as he usually did. As he crossed the road outside the school, a police car pulled out of the school drive. Karl noticed the car but kept walking, fearing to look at its occupants in case he aroused suspicion. The colleague of the police sergeant in the passenger seat gave Karl a hard look as the car pulled away.

As Karl passed Kayleigh's house, the shame of the events from the night before flooded his mind once again. He hurried passed her home and, as he entered his garden, looked back along the street in case she was in sight of him. He couldn't face her, knowing that a gang he was part of had caused such upset and injury to her family.

The empty house seemed almost haunting to Karl as he closed the door behind him. Although he had followed the same routine for several weeks, Karl still found it eerie to be on his own. He had never liked the feeling of loneliness. He called out to his mum and dad in the hope that someone was there for a change, but there was no reply. They were both out, living their separate lives as usual.

Karl threw his school bag down and went upstairs to change; then he returned to the kitchen to warm up his tea in the microwave oven. He watched part of a *Dr Who* DVD while eating his tea. Then, out of duty to his mum, he did the washing-up and some cleaning as he usually did to help her around the house.

An hour later, Karl was lying on his bed, staring at the ceiling. His homework was still in his school bag, untouched. The heavy rock music in the background was not helping him relax. He could not get the events of the day out of his mind, and the more he tried, the harder it was to forget about Kayleigh and her great-grandmother, or about Jed and his threats, and the forthcoming police interview.

The events of the night before also troubled him. He then thought about his friends. It was only a few months ago that Richie, Tommy, Andrew and Karl had been a group of friends on their own, causing no trouble – just fun-loving lads who did what they wanted. Kayleigh had also been a friend whom he had spent time with occasionally. Now he was lost in a gang that had brought knife culture to his school and his housing estate. Where had it all gone wrong? Karl wasn't sure, and he didn't really care. All he wanted to do was get out of the Gang and live a happy life again. Was it possible? Could it happen? He wished it already had.

Karl looked across the room to his alarm clock. It was almost 6.30 p.m. For the first time in a number of weeks, he was not getting ready to go out with the boys. In half an hour's time, the Gang would be meeting near the shopping centre in the middle of the estate. Although Karl did not enjoy being in the house on his own, he thought it a better option that night to stay in rather than go out and get into more trouble. No doubt, Jed and Cooper would call to find him. He would have to find an excuse not to go out that night. As he moved to sit on the edge of his bed, it came to him. His stomach was still sore after the beating they had given him at lunchtime. He could tell them he wasn't feeling well and needed to stay at home.

Karl switched on his computer and settled into a football game. He was hoping the game would take his mind off things, and, for a while, it did. Then he looked at the clock again. It read 7.15 p.m. The Gang would be together now – perhaps even on their way to call for him. He decided to stick to his plan and tell Jed he was not well enough to go out. Hopefully they would accept it and leave him alone that night. But what if they didn't?

As he thought of the consequences of turning against Jed, and the possibility of another bruising, his heart jumped a beat and he felt cold all over his body. Someone was ringing the doorbell!

CHAPTER SIX

As Karl entered the school grounds the next morning, he was met by Tommy and Andrew. They had been waiting for him at the school gates.

"And where were you last night?" asked Andrew.

"Er, I decided to 'ave a night in," said Karl.

"Pity! We called for you, to see if you wanted a game of footy," said Tommy.

Andrew smiled. "Don't look so worried, mate! It was only me bruv and me; Jed and Cooper didn't even come out! They must be really feeling it from the cops this time."

"What, you mean the Gang didn't meet up at all?" asked Karl, surprised by the news.

"Nope – only us and Richie," replied Andrew. "We had a kick-about. We thought you'd like to join us, but we couldn't get an answer."

"I thought it was Jed! That's why I didn't open the door," admitted Karl.

"He's got us all fearing him," said Tommy. "I hate being in the Gang! Always have done."

"He's turned even worse since his brother got done for drug dealing," said Andrew.

"Is he coming to school today?" asked Karl.

"What, with the cops still hanging around? What do you think?" replied Tommy.

"It may be the first day in ages that we enjoy ourselves," said Andrew. "I brought a football, so we can play at lunchtime."

Karl smiled. It was good to be with his two friends again, without any interference from Jed and Cooper.

Karl was enjoying a pressure-free morning without the Gang. Some of the other boys from the Gang were in school, but they made little noise or trouble without their leaders to influence them. Karl got his head down, started to work well in his lessons and took his mind off his troubles. Yet each time he saw Kayleigh in his class he felt uneasy. He tried to avoid her through the day, hoping she wouldn't ask any awkward questions.

The whole day was trouble-free. The police did not turn up, and no further interviews were given that day. Karl enjoyed spending time just with Richie, Tommy and Andrew, whilst the rest of the Gang did their own thing as well.

At the last bell of the day, the school occupants left to enjoy the weekend. For the first time in weeks, Karl was really looking forward to Saturday and Sunday.

As he proceeded home, Karl had the uneasy feeling that he was being followed. He looked over his shoulder several times, but he could see no one. As he opened the gate to his front garden, someone at the end of the street observed him, then walked away towards the main road.

Karl was relieved that the weekend had arrived. He was hoping to relax and enjoy himself over the two days off from school. He had no specific plans; he just wanted to chill out and take things easy.

Just after 7 p.m. the doorbell rang. Karl was lounging on the settee watching another DVD, and he was surprised to see both Paul and David standing on his doorstep when he looked through the front window.

"Hi," said Paul cheerfully when Karl answered the door.

"Uh, hi, Paul. What's up?"

Karl looked along the street in case any other members of the Gang were around. He didn't want Jed and Cooper to know he was talking to Paul and David.

"Well, David and I are on our way to the youth club. We were wondering if you'd like to come along as well?"

"Me!" gasped Karl.

"Yeah. We're having a meeting about a football match tomorrow," said David. "Mike has arranged for us to play against another church in an eleven-a-side game over on the rec, but we're short of a couple of players. He told us to invite anyone we know who may be interested in playing. If you come tonight, you may be able to get in the team for the match tomorrow."

"Oh!" said Karl. "Uh, I'm not sure, guys. I mean, I'm not the churchy type, you know. I don't feel right going to that kind of place."

"But we're only having a meeting about the game," Paul encouraged. "I told Mike you were really good at football. He said he'd like to meet you – especially when he learned you were a Liverpool fan."

Karl thought for a moment. The idea of playing on the rec was tempting, but he didn't like the idea of going to church. He also didn't want to chance being seen by any of the Gang. However, if he went with Paul and David, he could avoid Jed if he called for him, and also he would not be in the house alone.

"It's just about the game, right?" he asked.

"Yeah. As soon as everything is organised, you can go home – unless you want to stay," said Paul.

"Just give me a moment," said Karl.

Karl returned to the lounge, turned off the television and

picked up his jacket. As they left the house, he checked his mobile phone to see if he had received any messages.

As they entered the grounds of the church, a few minutes later, Karl was relieved that he had not seen anyone from the Gang. He still had no intention of staying after the meeting; but when he entered the church hall, he couldn't believe what he saw before him.

CHAPTER SEVEN

The church hall was alive with a range of activities. Karl vaguely remembered the room from his years in Sunday school, and, as he familiarised himself with the building again, he recognised most of the teenagers from school.

In one corner of the room, a group of girls were sitting chatting away, listening to an MP3 player. In the opposite corner, two boys were using a PlayStation. In the centre of the room, a pool table and a table-tennis table were both occupied. Paul noticed Mike and waved to him. Mike walked over and Paul introduced him to Karl.

"Hi, Karl," said Mike. "Glad to meet you. Paul and David have told me a lot about you."

"Have they?" asked Karl nervously.

He looked at Paul and David. They smiled back at him.

"Yeah. They told me you support Liverpool."

"Yeah, I do," said Karl.

"And that you're a good football player."

Karl shrugged his shoulders. "I'm not bad," he replied.

"Great! We've got a match tomorrow against another church from the town. I'm sure we'll be able to get you into the team. We're a few players short, so it's a good job you've come along."

Karl didn't know what to say. Mike made him feel needed somehow, as if the team were already depending on him. He was overwhelmed by the welcome he had received.

Mike called the team together for the meeting and led them into the chapel, which was connected to the hall by a short passageway. As Karl approached the door, he saw Kayleigh and Debbie standing talking in the kitchen, where refreshments were being served through a small hatch. Kayleigh and Debbie saw Karl and waved. As Karl waved back, Debbie whispered something to Kayleigh, who started to giggle in a silly manner. Karl wondered what had amused them so much as he sat down in the church for the meeting.

The meeting took only a few minutes. Mike gave out the details of the match to the players and made sure they all had a form which had to be signed by one of their parents to allow them to play. As the boys arose to return to the hall, Karl felt someone tap him on the shoulder.

"D'you fancy a game of pool?" asked David.

Karl had intended to leave straight after the meeting, but the youth club had begun to interest him.

"Yeah, OK," he replied.

Over an hour later, Karl, Paul and David had played each other at pool and were now playing table-tennis doubles with Mike. The last point was won by David and Paul, and Mike congratulated them on their victory. He then called everyone together into one group and, with his wife, Joanna, presented a small message from the Bible. Karl had no interest in hearing the message, but his attention was caught when Mike started to talk about loneliness and what the Bible says about it.

Mike explained that, as a Christian, a person is never alone because God promises to be with them always. He then related a story from his teenage years:

"My parents were always out and I had no brothers or sisters at home. I was always lonely at home, so I started to hang out with some guys from school just for something to do. But they were a bad lot. Before I knew it, I was smoking and drinking and getting into trouble with the police. I didn't think my life would ever change for the good.

"Then someone told me about the youth club at my local church. I started going and eventually I became a Christian. I gave up being with the gang, stopped smoking and drinking, and today I work within the Church as a minister.

"When I became a Christian, I felt that Jesus was real to me and that, somehow, I was never alone. If I ever began to feel lonely, I would look up the passages in my Bible that told me God was with me and then thank Him for His promises. I have never suffered loneliness since."

Karl realised that Mike had had a similar experience to his own. As Joanna closed the meeting with a small prayer, Karl began to feel a need to sort himself out just as Mike had done. He helped to clear the equipment away after the youth club finished, and he also did some cleaning-up. As he began to leave with Kayleigh, Debbie, David and Paul, Mike came up to him.

"It was good to meet you, Karl. I hope to see you tomorrow."

"I'll be there. Thanks for tonight."

"Pleasure. See you in the morning."

The friends said goodbye to one another and they went their separate ways. Karl walked with Kayleigh back to their street. Karl had had such a good time that he had forgotten all about his uneasiness with Kayleigh earlier in the day. As they walked home, Kayleigh smiled at him.

"Well, it was great to see you there tonight, Karl. I'm glad you came along."

"Thanks. It was Paul and David's idea, you know."

"Yes. They did mention they had talked to you about it. So you enjoyed it tonight, then?"

"Yes," admitted Karl, "I did actually."

"What are you doing after the match tomorrow?" asked Kayleigh.

"Nothing as far as I know, though I may be going over to my nan's at some stage."

"Well, some of us are going into town. You can join us if you'd like to."

Karl thought for a moment.

"Yeah, OK."

"Great! I'll see you tomorrow, then. Goodnight, Karl."

Kayleigh cheerfully opened her front door and waved to Karl as she closed it behind her.

As Karl walked back home, he felt that he was in a dream. Something special had happened that night – he could feel it. Perhaps his life was beginning to turn around after all!

CHAPTER EIGHT

Karl arose early the next morning in order to get ready for the football match. Although the team members were being provided with kit for the game, Karl still had to get a couple of things ready to take to the match. He also needed to get his mum to sign the form to allow him to play.

As he crossed the landing to the bathroom, he peeked into his mum and dad's room to see if she was awake. Usually, his mum had a lie-in on Saturday mornings. However, to his surprise, she wasn't in bed. Karl quickly went downstairs, hoping she had not gone to work to cover an extra shift. She hadn't. His mum was sitting in the kitchen drinking a cup of coffee, reading a magazine.

"Morning, Mum. Can you—"

"Where were you last night?" asked his mum angrily.

"I – I went out with some friends, that's all."

"You mean with that gang of yours."

"No – I went out with some other friends."

"Who?"

"Well – you don't know them – David and Paul, two lads in my class."

"So where did you go, then?" asked his mum, finishing her drink.

Karl hesitated. "We, er, we went to a youth club at the church."

"What! You at church? Don't make me laugh."

"It's true – honest. I've been asked to join the church football team. They're playing on the rec this morning. Can you sign this form to allow me to play?"

He handed his mum the form and she read it over.

"So that's what this is all about. I don't know if I should let you go," she replied.

"What d'you mean?" asked Karl.

"Sit down, Karl – we need to talk."

Karl took his seat opposite his mum and cautiously waited for her to begin.

"Your dad was on the way to the pub last night when two police officers turned up to speak to you."

"What did they want?" asked Karl nervously.

"They wanted to speak to you about the incident at that flat the other night. It seems they think you had something to do with it."

"But I didn't, I swear! I wouldn't do anything like that!"

"Maybe not, but Jed is a troublemaker – you know he is. It's just the sort of thing he'd do, isn't it?"

Karl kept silent.

"I want to know if you're in trouble or not?" ordered his mum.

"Mum, I didn't do anything – honest. The police came to the school. They've interviewed lots of boys from my year about it. It – it could have been anyone."

Karl knew that if he told the truth, his mum would never sign the form and he would be grounded. His mum gave a deep sigh and looked over the form again.

"I want you to stop hanging out with Jed's lot – do you understand me? They're nothing but trouble," she commented as she put her signature on the piece of paper.

"What about Tommy, Andrew and Richie?" asked Karl.

"They were good lads before they joined the Gang. You should leave them alone too until they decide to leave the Gang as well."

"But—"

"No buts! I don't want the police turning up here looking for you every night. I don't even know where you go these days. I know I work late, but you're never in in the evenings. I bet your school work is well behind."

"How do you know I'm not in?" protested Karl.

"Because I ring the house, that's why."

"You do?" asked Karl.

"Yes, I ring during my coffee break to make sure everything is all right. I know you're out with the Gang, and I know you're getting into trouble. It's time it stopped."

"Well, I wasn't with them last night," confirmed Karl.

"Good. Maybe that youth club will help you come to your senses. It's about time you started doing something different with your time!"

His mum handed him the form.

"Go on – get out of here. But if I hear of you getting into trouble, you'll be wishing Jed had done you over instead of me, you hear?"

"Yeah. Thanks, Mum!"

Karl went back upstairs and got ready for the match. He returned half an hour later, grabbed a piece of toast and ate it as he finished his preparations for the day ahead. As he left the house, his mum called to him:

"I'm going to your nan and grandad's at teatime. I want you to come over there to do some chores."

"But I was planning on going to town with the church group this afternoon," said Karl.

"You are taking this seriously, aren't you? OK, but make sure you come over afterwards."

"I will – promise. Thanks, Mum!"

Karl closed the door and hastily made his way to the rec for his first match for the church football team.

CHAPTER NINE

With five minutes to go, Karl's team were losing three goals to two. It had been a hard-fought game. Karl hadn't expected the other side to be as difficult to beat as they were. Some of the opposing players also played for school and local sides as well as their church. Karl was surprised at how competitive the game was.

Karl was used to playing in midfield, but he had to play where he could fit into the team. In the second half, he was playing off the front two strikers. Mike had made some changes at half-time and Karl was now in a much more comfortable role.

As Mike, Kayleigh, Debbie and some other church members cheered them on, Karl's team kept pressing for an equaliser. Karl picked up a loose ball near the halfway line and played a wonderful pass to David, who ran in on goal. Just as he was about to shoot, he was brought down by an opposing player. The referee blew his whistle and pointed to the spot. It was a penalty.

Mike looked across to the captain, Stephen Mills, and pointed to Karl. Stephen handed him the ball.

"It's all yours, Karl. You can do it."

Stephen had seen Karl play football in school and knew he was a good player. As Karl placed the ball on the penalty spot, Stephen walked to the outside of the area, confident that Karl would score. As Karl walked back to make his run, he looked across the field.

Mike, Kayleigh and Debbie cheered him on. "Come on, Karl! You can do it!" they shouted.

Karl made his run and placed the ball accurately to the goalkeeper's left, but the goalkeeper read the shot and dived in the same direction. He saved the penalty, but the force of the shot meant he did not hold on to it. Karl rushed forward and hit the rebound. The ball lifted up over the keeper and, to the defence's despair, rose into the net above him. Karl had scored the equaliser.

The final score was three all. The players from each side shook hands and agreed that a rematch should be played. Karl was exhausted, but he was happy that the team hadn't lost. It had been a great game.

A couple of hours later, Karl was in town with David, Paul, Kayleigh and Debbie. The girls were doing some shopping for some birthday banners for a party at the youth club for one of the members. The boys spent their time in the computer-games shops, trying out the latest games on the consoles there. After they had all finished, the party of friends ended up enjoying refreshments at a burger bar.

The afternoon went by quickly. They boarded the bus to return to the estate, and Karl prepared to leave them in order to get to his grandparents' home. When the time came, he rang the bell for the appropriate stop and got out of his seat.

"Thanks for today, guys," he said to them all. "It's been great."

"We've got an 'After Church' meeting tomorrow night, Karl. You're welcome to join us," said Paul.

"I might do that," said Karl, smiling at his new friend.

"I'll call for you tomorrow afternoon," suggested Kayleigh.

"Yeah, OK," replied Karl. "See you then."

Karl waited for the bus to pull away, and then he waved to his friends before crossing the road and making his way to his grandparents' home.

Having helped his mum with some gardening, Karl spent over an hour cleaning the windows around the bungalow while his mum did some extra chores inside. His grandfather was busy in his shed as usual, occasionally popping his head out of the doorway to see how Karl was doing.

As the evening began to draw in, Karl and his grandfather joined his mum and grandmother in the living room. When the time came for Karl and his mum to leave, his grandmother gave Karl a stern word regarding the news from the estate.

"I hear there's been some trouble with some boys on the estate, Karl."

"Uh, yeah, Nan, there has been."

"Poor Mrs Evans! I bet she's shaken up pretty badly."

"Yeah."

"They need locking up, these youngsters – always causing trouble. There was a break-in at the junior school along the road here two weeks ago, and someone vandalised the churchyard across the road." She pointed a long finger at Karl. "Now you listen, my boy! I don't want to hear of you getting into any trouble, you hear me?"

"Uh, yeah, Nan, I hear you."

"If you know anything about what happened, you make sure you tell the police. Just imagine if it had happened to me or your grandfather. How would you feel then, eh? Just because it was someone else's relative doesn't mean it's not important to catch the criminal!"

"We have to go now, Nan," said Karl, changing the subject quickly. "I'll see you next week."

He gave her a kiss on the cheek and followed his grandfather to the car.

As they pulled up at Karl's house, his grandfather turned to Karl, who was sat in the front passenger seat, and gave him a £10 note.

"That's for doing the windows," he said. "Don't spend it all at once!"

"Thanks, Gramps," said Karl.

His grandfather noticed that Karl was looking concerned about something. As his mum got out of the car, the old man put his hand on Karl's shoulder.

"Is everything all right, son?" he asked.

"Yeah, I think so."

"Something's up. I can tell by your face."

"Something Nan said just now," admitted Karl.

"What's that, then?"

"Well, I don't want to think any harm would come to the two of you."

"Oh, we're all right, Karl. Your nan was just making an example, that's all. Cheer up – nothing to worry about!"

"Yeah, I guess not," replied Karl. "Thanks for the money."

"That's OK. You did a good job. See you next week."

"Yeah. Bye, Gramps."

As Karl's mum began to cook some supper, Karl took his money upstairs and put it away in his savings box. He decided to put it towards his next computer game. He kept thinking about his grandmother's words, and he began to put himself in Kayleigh's shoes in his mind. How would he have felt if it had been his grandmother? It certainly made him think about what was fair to Kayleigh and her family. He was just beginning to plan what to do, when his mum called him for supper.

By the time the supper was eaten, it was almost 9.30 p.m.

"I'm going to listen to some music," said Karl.

"OK, love. I'll be up in a while," replied his mum.

Karl put his stereo on, and he was about to start up his computer to play some games when he had a change of mind. Being with his new friends had made him think about doing well in school again. Karl reached for his school bag and threw all of its contents on to the bed. He found the homework he needed to do for Monday and, leaving his bed covered in his school things, he went to his desk next to his computer and began his homework.

When his dad finally came home, there was a bit of noise which disturbed Karl from his studies. As his mum and dad came upstairs, they called goodnight to him and, after replying, Karl finished one piece of work before going to bed himself, just after midnight.

It had been a full but very rewarding day. Karl felt shattered but pleased that the day had gone so well. He fell asleep thinking of the football match he had played in and looking forward to the new day and being with his new friends again.

CHAPTER TEN

Meanwhile two figures were standing outside the petrol station on the estate, awaiting the arrival of another friend. Around them, the night life of the estate was in full swing. An engagement party was beginning to reach its climax at the local social club; last-minute meals were being purchased at the Chinese takeaway; landlords were clearing their premises of those who had spent the night drinking and socialising at their establishments; and, across the estate, taxis were dropping people home from town or collecting them for a final journey of the day.

As the shutters were brought down to cover the petrol-station windows and door, Jed and Cooper noticed Rogers approaching them along the main road. They made their way towards him and met him on the corner of a nearby avenue.

"Well, Rogers, any sign of 'im yet?" asked Jed.

Rogers shook his head. "He must be home – 'is bedroom light was on."

"So, the little rat stayed in. He didn't answer the door when we called for 'im," said Cooper.

Jed finished a can of lager, belched loudly, and threw the empty tin into a garden close by.

"And you're sure it was Edwards on the rec this mornin'?" Jed asked Rogers.

"I'm sure," answered Rogers firmly. "I saw 'im from the bus when I went into town."

Cooper looked at his best friend. "He's beginning to prove a bit of a problem, Jed."

"Yeah, he is. We'll have to show him who he really belongs to."

"D'you want me for anything else, Jed?" asked Rogers.

"No, mate. You go home. Thanks for your help."

"No problem. See you, Cooper."

Rogers ran off and disappeared into the night.

"What we gonna do about Edwards?" asked Cooper as the two boys started walking home.

"He's in for it big time. What we did to 'im in school is nothing to what we will do to 'im this time," answered Jed.

Cooper grinned nastily. "Another beating?" he questioned.

"Yeah, but first we're gonna do somethin' that'll make sure he stays loyal. Here's the plan. . . ."

Jed and Cooper talked all the way home and made their plans regarding Karl and the other boys in the Gang.

They were about to cross the main road to the street where they both lived when Cooper pulled Jed back to the kerb. A police car rushed past, its lights flashing, but without the sound of its siren. It was the third police car they had seen on their way home. Jed and Cooper followed the car with their eyes and watched it stop near the house of one of their friends.

Two women were fighting on the pavement outside their houses, and the police had been called by another neighbour. Moments later, a police car arrived from the other side of the estate.

"I hate the fuzz!" said Jed angrily, remembering the day his brother had been arrested.

Cooper watched the incident as they crossed the road.

"Looks like that woman next to Peters' house. She's always causing trouble."

Jed had walked on along their street, and he now stopped

outside his own house. He didn't have to look inside to know what was going on; he could hear it, and so could the rest of the residents in the street.

Jed's mum and dad were rowing in the living room. His mum had found out that his dad had taken some money from her purse and used it to gamble on the horses in the afternoon at the local betting shop. Then he had spent all his winnings at the local pub with his mates that night. He had turned up only a few minutes before Jed and Cooper, drunk, disorderly and broke. Jed could see several neighbours peering around their living-room curtains to see what was happening.

Suddenly there was an almighty breaking of glass, which set some dogs from the street barking at the noise.

"Any minute now and the fuzz will be 'ere!" said Jed.

"Come on, Jed – come to my house for a bit," suggested Cooper.

Jed shook his head. "I wanna know what's happening," he said.

Another police car could be heard approaching the area.

"Come on, Jed," said Cooper firmly. "We don' wanna get spotted by the cops!"

Reluctantly, Jed followed Cooper to Cooper's house. They entered his garden and crouched behind a fence out of sight of the arriving police, but still within viewing distance to find out what was happening. Moments later, Jed found out. A police car turned up and two officers went to Jed's front door. Minutes later, his dad was led away by the officers to spend the night in a cell, in order to calm down. Jed stood up as the car left the street, and he saw his dad in the back of the vehicle.

"I'm going 'ome," he said to Cooper.

He was just stepping out of Cooper's garden when his mum left their house and closed the door behind her. She walked to the end of the street and crossed the main road, oblivious to both Jed and Cooper, who were watching her leave.

"Where's your mum going?" asked Cooper.

"My auntie's, I expect," replied Jed.

"You gonna be OK on your own?"

Jed laughed. "Best time to be in the house! I'll be fine, mate. I'll see you tomorrow."

Jed walked the few yards back to his own house, leaving Cooper to himself.

When he entered, Jed found the living-room lights still on. The room was in a mess. Newspapers and magazines had been thrown everywhere. Glasses were broken and drinks had been spilled across the furniture and carpet.

When Jed entered the kitchen, he found the reason behind the sound of smashed glass. The kitchen window had a huge hole in the middle of it, where his dad had thrown a hammer at the glass and broken it. Jed uncaringly turned from the window and walked across the kitchen to the fridge. He opened the fridge door and took a can of lager for himself. He opened the can and began to guzzle down the drink as he walked back through the house, turning the lights off before climbing the stairs to his bedroom in total darkness.

He closed the door behind him and locked it. His brother had fitted the lock to his door when he had been living at home, to protect him from his father's violence. Only Jed and his brother had a key to it. Once it was locked, his mum and dad could not get in. Jed always felt secure in the room thanks to his brother's help.

He walked across the room, which was illuminated only by the street light outside the house, and opened the window. More sirens and arguments could be heard close by. Jed took the knife out of his pocket and, lying on his bed, reached underneath it for a small tin. He opened the tin and placed the knife inside.

He lay on his bed for a while, then finished the can of lager he had taken from the fridge, thinking all the time about his plans for Karl and the Gang. He picked up the tin again and grinned.

"You're mine, Edwards! You're all mine!" he said quietly to himself.

Then he fell asleep, listening to the estate's symphony of sound as another Saturday night came to an end.

CHAPTER ELEVEN

Karl arrived at school on Monday morning in a cheerful mood. The weekend had been a great success as far as he was concerned. After all the events of Saturday, Karl had finished his homework on Sunday afternoon before attending the evening service and the 'After Church' meeting with his new friends. He was mostly thankful that the weekend had passed without any involvement with Jed and the Gang. Since going to the youth club on Friday evening, Karl had realised there were alternatives to the life he had. He knew there were better ways of spending his time than getting into trouble on the estate.

Approaching the school gates, he saw Richie and Andrew walking further ahead of him, and he ran to catch them up.

"Hi, guys. What's up?" he asked with a large smile on his face.

Neither Richie nor Andrew spoke to him. They stopped, looked him sadly in the eye, then walked on ahead of him.

Karl was mystified. Why were they ignoring him? Had he done something wrong? He caught them up again to find out.

"Hey! What's going on?" he asked. "Why aren't you talking to me?"

Richie looked over his shoulder, checking to see if any other members of the Gang were about. Seeing that none of them were in sight, he looked at Andrew and nodded.

"We've been warned off from hanging out with you," answered Andrew.

"Why?" asked Karl. "Has Jed warned you off?"

"Yeah, he has," Andrew replied. "He reckons you are being disloyal to the Gang, so no one is allowed to have any more to do with you."

"But what have I done to make him think that?" asked Karl.

"Rogers saw you playing football at the rec on Saturday," replied Richie. "Then you didn't come out when Jed called for you on Saturday evening."

Karl sighed. He hadn't anticipated being seen by anyone from the Gang whilst he had been playing football for the church team.

"I was playing football for the youth club team," he admitted.

"What, the youth club from the church?" asked Andrew.

Karl nodded in reply.

"No wonder Jed is worked up with you," said Richie. "What made you do a thing like that? You know Jed hates the church and anyone who goes to the youth club!"

"Paul and David asked me to join the team. They were a couple of players short for a match on Saturday morning. I didn't think there would be any trouble over it."

"What about Saturday evening?" asked Andrew.

"I was out on Saturday evening," answered Karl. "I went to my nan's. I had to do some chores over there for my mum. We didn't get back 'til late."

The boys arrived at the main school building and went to one of the toilet blocks. Karl had noticed when he had met Richie and Andrew that Tommy wasn't with them as usual, but he had been distracted from asking where he was by talking about his own weekend.

"Hey, Andy, where's your brother?" Karl asked as he washed his hands.

Andrew didn't know how best to tell Karl the news about his brother, so he just came straight out with the answer.

"He's in hospital, Karl," replied Andrew sadly.

"What!" gasped Karl. "Why? What happened?"

"It's a long story," said Richie, who then gave Karl all the details.

Whilst Karl had been studying on Sunday afternoon, Jed had called the Gang together for a game of football. He had tackled Tommy roughly, and, after Tommy had landed on the ground, both Jed and Cooper had deliberately stamped on his right leg, causing a fracture. Then they continued to kick him while Tommy lay there in agony. Richie and Andrew had called for help after the other boys had run off. Tommy had been taken to hospital and would be staying in for a few days.

"Why didn't you let me know last night?" asked Karl. "You could have texted me."

"Because", replied Andrew, "Jed told us that if we said anything to you he'd do the same to us!"

"He'll probably do something to us if he finds out we've been talking to you now," suggested Richie.

Andrew looked at him worriedly.

"So you're not going to speak to me any more, or hang out with me ever again, then?" Karl asked.

Andrew sighed. He looked at Richie and then at Karl.

"Look, Karl, it's not that we don't want to hang out with you or anything. It's just that, well . . ."

Andrew paused and Richie took over the conversation:

"You weren't there yesterday when Jed and Cooper attacked Tommy, Karl. They went crazy. We've never seen Jed get so angry."

Karl briefly remembered the beating Jed and Cooper had given him the week before. They had obviously been worse towards Tommy.

"We do want to hang out with you," continued Richie, "but they've really got it in for us this time. To be honest, we're both scared to death of Jed and Cooper!"

"And Rogers as well!" added Andrew. "He joined in with them when they kicked Tommy."

"We don't want to cross their path in case they do something worse to us," said Richie.

"And you think Jed and Cooper will if we stay friends, is that it?" asked Karl.

"D'you think they won't?" asked Andrew. "They'll do something to us if they know we're still talking to you. You know what they're like, Karl."

"Yeah, I know what they're like," replied Karl reflectively.

The boys became quiet when another boy entered the toilets. Until he left, they pretended to be getting ready for registration. Then Karl spoke to his two friends:

"What if we leave the Gang and go back to just the four of us hanging out together, like before?" he asked firmly.

"What?" gasped Andrew. "You think that will stop them? They'd find us and do something far worse if we did that!"

"So you really want to carry on hanging out with them, then?"

"No," said Richie, "we don't, but what other option is there?"

"I don't know," admitted Karl, "but we can't carry on like this – any of us. We're all being ruled by fear. It can't go on any more."

The bell for registration suddenly rang throughout the school. Karl checked his watch.

"Look," he said after a brief moment, "you two had better get to class without me. If we turn up at different times, there's less chance that Jed will suspect we've been talking to each other."

"What are we going to do about the Gang?" asked Richie.

"I don't know, but I think I can speak to someone I know about it. I'll see you later. Now get going."

Richie and Andrew said their farewell to Karl and walked off to registration, leaving Karl on his own. As Karl began to make a move for registration, his thoughts turned to Mike from the church.

'Perhaps he could help us,' thought Karl.

Karl realised he couldn't deny playing on the rec for the church football team. Rogers had seen him. Saturday evening had not been his fault. He had genuinely got home late from visiting his grandparents. Even if he had wanted to go out with the Gang, he had arrived home too late to catch up with them.

Karl knew he would have to face Jed soon. What would he say to him? How would Jed react? How could Richie, Andrew, Tommy and he continue their friendship now that Jed had got in the way of them hanging out together?

Karl was not looking forward to the rest of the day. He arrived outside his registration room, braced himself and opened the door.

CHAPTER TWELVE

Jed, Cooper and Rogers were not in school that morning. They were staying away in case of any further police trouble. Karl felt relieved when he noticed they were not present in registration. Karl also observed some of the other boys from the Gang whispering to each other and pointing at him. He ignored them and sat on his own, near the front of the classroom. Some of the other members of the form, including Kayleigh, felt that there was an uneasiness in the room. They wondered what was happening between Karl and the other boys from the Gang.

The morning passed without any trouble. Karl settled into his lessons and focused on his work rather than allowing himself to be distracted by the other boys.

At lunchtime, Karl went to the school canteen alone. Andrew and Richie noticed Karl buying sandwiches instead of a cooked meal as usual. He left the canteen before any of the boys from the Gang could catch up with him. He suspected that they would hassle him over his disloyalty, so he decided to stay out of their way.

Karl found a quiet spot on the school grounds to eat his lunch, then went to the library, where he was able to do some studying. He knew that none of the Gang would go to the library. Jed would be as worked up with them as he was with Karl if they did. For a while, at least, he knew he was safe.

Karl hadn't realised that he had been followed, though! As he took a seat at an available desk and opened his bag to take out the work he wanted to do, Kayleigh and Debbie entered the library. They sat down opposite Karl. Karl looked up, acknowledged them both, and went back to his studies.

Kayleigh took a small notepad out of her bag and scribbled a quick message on one of its pages. She then tore the page off and passed it across the table to Karl, taking care not to let the teacher on duty see what she was doing. Karl picked up the message, slipped it inside his book and read it.

The message read, 'Are you all right?'

Karl decided to tell Kayleigh the truth. He tore a page out of his A4 notepad and wrote a quick summary of what Richie and Andrew had told him that morning. Kayleigh and Debbie were upset and angered by his words. They were annoyed that Jed had treated Karl and his friends so badly because Karl had gone to the youth club.

Kayleigh wrote another message, telling Karl she would call for him after school. As the note was handed to Karl, the teacher walked past and stopped to help a student with a query. The three friends did some work for the rest of the lunchtime, without any more messages being passed between them.

Karl had only just settled into the first lesson of the afternoon when there was an interruption to the class. The burly figure of Sergeant Haynes entered the room. The boys from the Gang shuddered when they saw him. The police were back at the school, as Jed had anticipated they would be – only this time he was not there to help them face the situation.

"I would like the following boys to come with me, please," he ordered.

Several names were read out, including Richie's and Karl's. The other boys from the Gang watched as the Sergeant led them out of class towards the interview room, wondering what each of them would say to the police.

The Sergeant led them to a small office. None of the boys dared speak whilst they followed. Karl didn't know what he was going to say; neither did Richie. Yet, surprisingly, they looked a lot calmer than the other boys from the Gang who had been called out with them.

Collins was led into the office to be interviewed first. A teacher sat with the other boys outside the interview room so there was no opportunity for them to converse with one another. Karl sat in silence, not looking at the other boys, and pondered what he would say. He remembered what his grandmother had told him on Saturday evening – to tell the truth if he knew anything. Then his thoughts turned to Tommy in hospital. He didn't want anything to happen to Richie or Andrew, so could he risk saying anything about what had happened on the estate?

After approximately ten minutes, Collins emerged from the room, looked at the boys and returned to his class. Davison was interviewed next, followed by Peters, then Richie. Despite his name being near the top of the register, Karl was left until last to be interviewed. When his turn finally arrived, Karl stepped into the small office and sat down at the instruction of the Sergeant.

"This is PC Hall," Sergeant Haynes explained, indicating the young female officer who was sat next to him. "She will be conducting this interview, Karl."

PC Hall had visited the youth club at the church several weeks before. She had been working on the estate for approximately six months and had a good idea of the problems people were facing in the area. Unknown to Karl, she was a Christian; she attended a church in the city centre with her husband.

PC Hall confirmed Karl's personal details, then began with the main questioning:

"Now, Karl, although this is called an interview, I don't want you to get uptight or uneasy with either Sergeant Haynes or myself. We want to ask you a few questions, and I hope you will be able to assist us with our inquiries."

Karl began to feel a little uneasy, despite the officer's introductory words.

"Do you go out with any friends or socialise with anyone on the estate?" continued PC Hall.

Karl hesitated. 'If I tell them about going to the youth club, it may throw them off asking about the Gang,' he thought to himself.

"Sometimes I do," he replied.

"Where do you go, Karl? Anywhere specific?"

"I've started going to the youth club at the church," admitted Karl.

"Ah, so you know Mike and Joanna, then?" asked PC Hall.

"Yeah, do you?" asked Karl, surprised that the policewoman had brought up their names.

PC Hall explained that she had been to the youth club to speak to the teenagers about the problems of knife crime and the gang culture on the estate.

"I don't remember seeing you when I spoke there a few weeks ago," said the officer.

"I've – I've only just started going. David and Paul invited me last Friday. I played for their football team on Saturday at the rec."

Sergeant Haynes was making his own notes as the interview continued.

"Do you go out much with Paul and David?" PC Hall asked.

"Not really. I've only just started hanging out with them," admitted Karl.

"Oh, why is that?"

Karl wasn't sure what to say. Should he admit to being in the Gang or should he keep quiet about Jed?

"Well, my mum and dad are out a lot in the evenings," he explained. "It gets lonely sometimes at home. They seem to be all right to hang out with, so I started going to the youth club."

"OK, so we know you attend the youth club. Is there anyone else you hang out with?" asked PC Hall.

"Well, I used to hang out with three lads from my class," Karl explained.

"Who are they, Karl?" asked Sergeant Haynes.

"Tommy and Andrew Young and Richie Thomas," replied Karl.

"Ah, we've just spoken to Richie. He told us that Tommy broke his leg yesterday playing football."

"Yes, Andrew told me this morning."

"You mean you weren't there with them when it happened?"

"No, I was doing some homework."

Sergeant Haynes did not let up with his questioning.

"We've also been told by another one of your classmates that you hang out with Jed and his gang."

The Sergeant's statement pushed Karl into a corner he knew he couldn't get out of. Yet Karl wasn't surprised. What better way for the Gang to get back at him than to try to get him into trouble with the police!

"Well, I used to," said Karl.

"What does that mean?" asked the Sergeant.

Karl looked into a dark corner of the small office and decided to tell the truth. He explained what had happened over the weekend: that he had been a part of Jed's gang, but, after going to the youth club, Jed had told the boys to have nothing more to do with him. He was now an outcast as far as the Gang was concerned.

The two officers looked at each other for a moment and shared some comments quietly. PC Hall then continued with the questions:

"Karl, we've been told by another member of the Gang that Jed caused the incident with Mrs Evans last week. Do you know if that is true?"

PC Hall's comment took Karl by surprise. Was she saying it just to get him to confess, or had someone truly given Jed away?

"I – I wasn't with them when it happened," said Karl truthfully.

"Where were you, then?" asked Sergeant Haynes.

"I called into the garage to buy a drink. The rest of the Gang walked on ahead of me. By the time I left the shop, they were halfway up the hill. I didn't catch up with them."

"But you were in the area when it happened," suggested the Sergeant.

"I heard the glass smash, but I didn't see what actually happened," said Karl honestly.

"Do you think Jed could have done it?" asked PC Hall.

Karl didn't reply. He wasn't sure what to say in answer to her question.

"Well, Karl?" asked PC Hall.

Still silence – Karl said nothing. He just sat there and looked into the corner of the room again, thinking about Tommy lying in hospital.

"Karl, answer the question, please," ordered Sergeant Haynes.

"Why do I need to answer it if someone has already given Jed away?" asked Karl sharply.

"Well," replied PC Hall, "we haven't been able to confirm his statement. The more evidence we have against Jed from people like yourself, the better the case is against him."

"Helping us with our enquiries could help you in the long run," said Sergeant Haynes. "Just think how much easier things will be without him around to cause trouble."

"But I didn't see anything," protested Karl. "I was so far

behind them all, I didn't see what happened."

PC Hall suspected there was another reason why Karl wasn't answering the question directly.

"Does Jed bully you at all, Karl?" she asked.

"What?" asked Karl.

"Does he threaten you – you know, if you say anything, he'll do something to you? That type of thing."

Karl looked her straight in the eyes. He felt as though she could almost read his mind and find out that way what Jed was like.

"Is Jed threatening you, to stop you from saying anything?" she asked.

Karl felt his facial expression change and he knew it had given away the truth.

"You are being bullied by Jed, aren't you?" asked PC Hall.

Karl decided to admit the truth. He nodded. "They beat me up last week," he admitted.

"Why did they do that, Karl? You're meant to be one of their friends."

"I was talking to David and Paul after games. Jed very often picks on Paul in the changing room. He thought I was being disloyal by hanging out with them, so he and Cooper had a go at me."

"You mean Adrian Cooper?" asked the Sergeant.

Karl nodded in agreement. The Sergeant rummaged though a folder and produced a photograph of Jed's closest friend.

"Is this the character, Karl?" he asked, showing Karl the photograph.

"Yeah. He's Jed's best mate. They always hang out together," Karl said.

"Did you tell anyone that they beat you up when it happened?" asked Sergeant Haynes.

Karl shook his head. "No – kept it to myself."

"So you're afraid that if you say anything more, Jed will do the same to you again?" he asked.

"No, I'm not afraid of what they'll do to me. I'm more concerned they'll do something to either Richie or Andy. Jed threatened he'd do worse to them than he did to Tommy if they had anything more to do with me."

"You mean Jed broke Tommy's leg deliberately to get back at you for being disloyal to him?" asked PC Hall.

"That's the way I see it. The four of us were best friends before joining the Gang. Now Jed has stopped us hanging out together."

Sergeant Haynes and PC Hall again spoke quietly to each other.

"OK, Karl, at least you have confirmed one thing we are investigating," said the Sergeant. "We are also following up reports of Jed's behaviour towards certain individuals in the class. That's a start at least. I think we can let you return to your class for now; but if you do feel you want or need to say anything further to us, tell one of your teachers and we can come back and speak to you."

PC Hall gave Karl a card with some phone numbers on it.

"If you ever need to talk to someone, we have a support group to help victims of bullying. You can call them at any time, day or night," she explained.

"Thanks," said Karl.

"And if anything does arise that you need to talk to us about," she added, "this is our phone number at the station. You can also contact someone there any time."

Karl picked up his school bag from the floor, inserted the card PC Hall had given him into a pocket on its side, and left the office to return to class.

In the dimly lit office, Karl had lost track of time. He checked his watch and realised he only had one lesson left for the day, and that had already started. He made his way to the classroom quickly, thinking over all he had said to the police. Had he said anything that would cause further trouble with Jed? Who had revealed that Jed had committed the crime against Mrs Evans? Would there ever be a solution to the problems Karl was facing?

He looked up to a corner of the ceiling in the corridor and found himself, surprisingly, praying.

"God, if You are there," he prayed quietly, "please sort this mess out."

As he entered the classroom, Karl had no idea how important those words would be.

CHAPTER THIRTEEN

Mike was making preparations for a sermon for the forthcoming Sunday when the interruption happened. Sat at his desk, he had just taken a sip from a fresh cup of coffee when he felt the Lord speak to him about the problems faced by some of the members of the youth club on the estate and in school. Knowing he was being encouraged to pray, Mike set his cup down and laid his notes to one side. Focusing his mind, he closed his eyes and began to meditate on what the Holy Spirit was showing him. Moments later, he was praying for all the members of the youth club – especially for Karl, Kayleigh, Debbie, David and Paul.

Mike was not the only one sensing the need for prayer. At the Ladies' Society in the church hall, Joanna felt the Lord urge her to ask the ladies present to pray for the young people. Following her prayer, she changed the address she was going to use and spoke instead about youth work connected with the church, highlighting the main needs the young people had and the circumstances they were facing in school and on the estate. She ended her talk by asking the ladies to pray regularly for the young people and the members of the church who worked with them.

PC Hall was also feeling the need to pray. As she waited alongside Sergeant Haynes, who was talking to the headmaster about the interviews they had conducted that day, PC Hall was silently praying for the boys she had interviewed that afternoon – particularly for Richie, Andrew and Karl.

The whole class turned to look at Karl as he entered the room. Mr Barnes, the art teacher, acknowledged Karl and pointed to an available chair next to Kayleigh. Karl crept quietly through the room and took his seat. After Mr Barnes had finished addressing the class, he approached Karl.

"Sorry I'm late, sir," said Karl. "I've been—"

"Yes, I've heard," replied Mr Barnes, looking at Kayleigh.

Karl realised from his expression that Kayleigh had told his teacher the reason for his absence.

"You missed the beginning of my explanation for this project, Karl, so I'll let your friends bring you up to speed. I've decided to offer this class the chance to work on after school tomorrow as there are a number who are behind in their work – including yourself, I might add."

Karl reached into his school bag and pulled out his sketchbook. He handed it to Mr Barnes.

"What's this?" asked his teacher.

"My homework, sir," Karl replied.

"You mean you've done it? My, my! Miracles do happen! OK, I'll give it a look-over and let you have it back at the end of the lesson."

As Mr Barnes walked back to his desk, Karl looked across the room and saw Richie and Andrew sitting together. Richie smiled at him, but Andrew had a solemn face. Karl wondered why Andrew seemed to be so down and assumed it was to do with Tommy.

Kayleigh and Debbie explained what the new project entailed, and Karl got up to collect the materials he needed for the lesson. Even when Karl walked past him to collect what he needed, Andrew still didn't acknowledge him. Karl sensed that there was something very wrong with Andrew, but his gesturing to Richie to find out what availed him nothing. Karl got on with his work, hoping he would get the opportunity to speak to his friend after school to see what the problem was.

Art was always enjoyable, and Karl soon forgot about his troubles with the Gang and with the police as he proceeded with his artwork.

As the final bell of the day rang, Mr Barnes handed back the homework he had marked, and he addressed the whole class.

"Don't forget to let your parents know if you are staying on tomorrow, and don't forget this week's homework assignment," he ordered.

He then came to Karl and handed him back his sketchbook, which was now fully marked.

"This is excellent, Karl. You've produced some very good-quality work. It's about time you showed what you can do. Keep this standard up and you'll get a very high grade in your assessment."

"Thank you, sir," said Karl, who was happy to receive his teacher's encouraging comments.

Taking his sketchbook, Karl glanced across the table and saw Kayleigh beaming at him with pride.

"Do you think you will be able to stay after school tomorrow to catch up with your other project work?" asked Mr Barnes.

Kayleigh spoke up encouragingly. "Debbie and I are going to stay on," she said.

Karl smiled at her and turned back to Mr Barnes.

"Yes, sir, I'll be here."

"Good lad! I'll see you tomorrow. Keep up the good work."

Mr Barnes smiled at Karl and Kayleigh, then walked off to the staffroom.

Kayleigh leaned over the desk.

"Let's have a look, then," she said joyfully, pointing to Karl's sketchbook.

Before he knew what was going on, Kayleigh was showing

Debbie the work Karl had completed over the weekend. As the two girls looked at his work, Karl looked out for Andrew and Richie. They had already left the room without even saying goodbye to him.

"That's really good," said Debbie, handing Karl his book and distracting him from his thoughts.

"What? Oh, thanks," said Karl, taking the book from her.

Kayleigh noticed Karl looking for his two friends.

"Are you OK, Karl?" she asked.

"Yeah, I guess so," said Karl, sighing. "I was hoping to catch Andy. He looked really miserable all lesson."

"He got called to speak to the police at lunchtime," explained Debbie.

"Oh, I didn't know that," said Karl.

"I heard him telling Richie when we came to art," she continued.

"You can walk home with us for a change," said Kayleigh, nudging Debbie's arm.

"Uh, yeah, actually we've been meaning to talk to you about something," said Debbie.

Karl's mind was still focused on Andrew and Richie, but he took in what Debbie had said.

"Yeah? What's that, then?" he asked.

"Well, some of the members of the youth club are meeting at the church later to discuss a design for a new Sunday-school banner. Why not come along? I'm sure you can come up with some good ideas for it."

"We could really do with your help, Karl," added Kayleigh.

"Well, I was going to try to catch up with some more school work, but I guess I could take a break and call over," he said, picking up his school bag.

"Great! We're meeting about 7 p.m.," Kayleigh explained.

"I should be finished by then anyway," said Karl.

"OK, I'll call for you on the way to Debbie's," suggested Kayleigh.

"Yeah, OK," replied Karl.

Karl, Kayleigh and Debbie left the school, talking about the ideas for the banner that members of the youth club had already come up with. Karl became interested in the project and, as he entered his home that evening, he made up his mind to get his homework done ready for another night out at the church.

CHAPTER FOURTEEN

Karl was finishing off a piece of homework when Kayleigh called for him. They had agreed to meet early so that Karl could avoid running into anyone from the Gang on the way to the meeting. Once Kayleigh arrived, the two of them set off and made their way to Debbie's house, which was opposite the church.

After arriving at Debbie's house, Kayleigh and Debbie chatted about a number of things, none of which interested Karl. He simply stood by the living-room window and peered round the corner of the curtain to keep an eye on what was happening on the estate. Although everything seemed peaceful, Karl had an uneasy feeling it was not going to remain that way for very long.

Meanwhile, Jed and Cooper were meeting other members of the Gang at the shopping centre. Jed had been in a foul mood ever since Rogers told him that Karl and Richie had been interviewed by the police. His mood had worsened when the police turned up at his house to interview him; and on top of that Jed's dad was furious with him for causing the police to go to the family home. When the officers had left, Cooper heard the rowing between Jed and his father from his own house three doors away.

When Jed met the Gang, he instantly noticed that Andrew, Karl and Richie were not with them and his temper reached boiling point.

"Anyone know where those three traitors are?" he asked forcefully.

Most of the boys shook their heads, but Williams made a comment:

"They were in art together last lesson. P'raps they've arranged to do something tonight."

"They'd better not 'ave," Jed bellowed. He pointed at Williams and Powell. "You two," he ordered, "get over to Edwards' house and find out where he is." Then he nodded to two others. "Davison, Peters, you go and call for Young. We'll meet back 'ere in 'alf an hour. You'd better bring them back with you, or else!"

But neither party were able to fulfil Jed's wishes. Williams and Powell got no answer from Karl's house, and Davison and Peters received no answer at Andrew's.

"Perhaps they've both gone to Richie's," suggested Rogers.

"Let's go and find out," said Jed menacingly.

Karl, Kayleigh and Debbie were just about to leave the house when Debbie spotted the Gang walking up the hill towards the church.

"Quickly! Get inside!" she ordered.

Karl and Kayleigh did as they were told. Debbie entered the living room and watched as the Gang passed by. She observed them as they made their way towards the other side of the estate. Debbie gave Karl the all-clear and he opened the front door again.

"Where are they going?" Kayleigh asked Karl.

"Probably to call for Richie," replied Karl. "I'd better text him to let him know they're on their way."

Ensuring that the Gang was out of sight, Karl, Kayleigh and Debbie made their way across the road to the church. Karl sent a text message to Richie, warning him of the Gang's approach, then entered the meeting.

Richie was playing a football game on his computer when the text message arrived from Karl. Richie was so focused on the game that he didn't hear the phone's message alert tone.

After getting home that evening, Richie had wanted to relax and forget about the day. He had found the police interview very stressful, and he just wanted to chill out instead of going out on the estate that night. So when the front doorbell rang he didn't answer it immediately. Only after it had rung for the fifth time did he pause his game and leave his bedroom to answer the door.

"Jed!" cried Richie, pulling the front door open.

"Who were you expecting – the Avon lady?" asked Jed.

Richie became very frightened. He was scared of what Jed was going to do.

"Why have you stayed in? We met up nearly an hour ago!"

Richie looked for an excuse that Jed would accept.

"I – I – sorry, Jed. I lost track of time – honest!"

"Are Edwards and Young with you?" asked Cooper.

"What? Uh, no. I haven't seen them since school," replied Richie nervously.

"Get your jacket. You're coming out with us now!" ordered Jed.

Richie fearfully went back to his room, turned his computer off and collected his jacket. In his rush to please Jed, he forgot to pick up his mobile phone.

Richie's house was close to one of the two primary schools on the estate. Jed led the boys towards the school. He pulled himself up over the railings and jumped down on to the school grounds.

"Come on, you lot – I 'aven't got all night!"

The rest of the Gang followed one by one, and soon they were all following Jed across the grounds of the school to the far side of the building, which could not be seen from the road or any of the nearby houses. Jed lit a cigarette and turned to Richie.

"Rogers 'ere", he said, pointing to his friend, "tells me that you and Edwards both saw the fuzz today."

"Uh, yeah, we did," replied Richie nervously, "but so did Davison, Peters and Collins."

The three boys Richie mentioned looked sinisterly at him.

"I'm not interested in anyone else – just you and Edwards!" said Jed.

Jed nodded to Cooper, who took hold of Richie and pulled him up against the wall of the school. Jed took his jacket off, rolled up the sleeves of his sweatshirt and closed in on Richie.

"So, what did you tell the fuzz, Thomas?"

Richie swallowed fearfully, gathered his thoughts and thought back to his interview.

"Nothing, Jed – honest!"

Jed swore, threw his cigarette to the ground and thrust the lower part of his left arm into Richie's face.

"You must have said something!" he argued. "I had the fuzz up my 'ouse two hours ago, askin' all sorts of questions. After they left, the ol' man did this to me!"

Richie could not help noticing a number of circular burn marks on Jed's arm. They were roughly the size of a cigarette end. Richie guessed what had happened to Jed. When Cooper also saw the marks, he realised what all the noise in Jed's house had been about.

"I'm sorry, Jed," replied Richie, looking at the marks on Jed's arm, "but I really didn't say anything. Honest I didn't!"

"You must have said something to send the fuzz up my 'ouse!"

"They asked me if I knew you and I said yes, but I didn't say anything wrong – 'onest!"

Jed raised a fist, intending to intimidate Richie into telling the truth.

"One more chance: what did you say?"

"Nothing!" Richie cried. Jed was about to hit him when Richie added, "But someone else did!"

Jed pushed his left arm across Richie's throat and drew his right fist back, ready to throw a punch.

"What d'you mean 'Someone else did'?"

Richie was remembering what Sergeant Haynes had told him.

"The cops told me someone had already given them information about what you did to the flat last week. They wanted me to confirm it, but I said I didn't see anything, I swear!"

Jed lowered his hands and let Richie go. Something in Richie's voice made Jed believe him.

Cooper spoke up: "It must have been Edwards, then!" he concluded.

Richie shook his head. "It wasn't Karl. He was interviewed after me."

Jed turned to the three boys who had been interviewed at the same time as Richie and Karl that afternoon.

"Is Richie telling the truth? Were Thomas and Edwards the last to be interviewed?"

The three boys were silent. Then Peters said reluctantly, "Yeah, they were."

"So, it's one of you three!" Jed bellowed.

Before Davison, Peters or Collins could do anything about it, Jed had punched Davison in the face. When he hit the ground, Jed turned to Peters, who was being held by Rogers, and lashed out at him. Collins tried to make a run for it, but Cooper jumped on him and wrestled him to the ground. As the rest of the Gang looked on, Jed gave each of the three boys a piece of his anger before letting them go.

After the roughing-up was over, Jed faced the Gang and gave his orders.

"If any of you say anything more to the fuzz, you'll get a lot worse than what these three 'ave 'ad! Do I make myself clear?"

The boys nodded in agreement. They knew Jed meant what he said.

Jed then turned to Cooper and Rogers.

"I have another score to settle tonight. Come on – we've got work to do." Jed turned to the rest of the Gang. "The rest of you had better find out what happened to Edwards and Young, or there will be trouble tomorrow for all of you!"

Jed, Cooper and Rogers left the school premises and made their way to the bus stop, leaving the rest of the Gang to themselves for the rest of the evening. As the boys climbed back over the railings, Peters grabbed Richie and pulled him back.

"Well, thanks for nothing!" he said coldly.

"What? I didn't know what Jed was going to do!" protested Richie.

"Well, I didn't give him away!" argued Peters.

"Neither did I," said Collins, rubbing his sore cheekbone.

"I didn't say anything either," added Davison.

The other boys from the Gang were looking on.

"Well," said Williams, "one of you must have. You were all seen by the cops."

The argument continued between the boys as they returned to the shopping centre to continue their search for Karl and Andrew.

CHAPTER FIFTEEN

Karl had turned his mobile phone off during the meeting. When he switched it back on after the meeting had ended, he received a surprising text message: 'Gang looking 4 u 4 Jed. Stay off the estate.'

The message was anonymous, but Karl recognised Richie's number. He had gone back to get his phone before going to look for Karl and Andrew with the Gang.

Kayleigh looked at Karl and saw that something was concerning him.

"What's the matter?" she asked as she approached him from across the hall.

Karl showed her the text message.

Kayleigh's stomach turned. Then, with her customary quickness of mind, she snatched Karl's phone and, before Karl could stop her, she was showing Joanna the message.

Mike was talking to a couple of members of the church when Joanna caught his attention. He said goodnight to the people he had been talking to and turned to his wife.

"Something the matter?" he asked curiously.

She nodded and showed him the message.

Mike read the message and looked across the room at Karl. He knew exactly what to do.

"Tell Kayleigh we'll give her and Karl a lift home," he said.

When Karl found out he was going to have a lift home, he became annoyed with Kayleigh.

"You had no right to show them that message!" he protested. Mike overheard the sentence.

"What's the matter? Don't you want a lift home?" he asked.

Karl turned to look at him. Everyone had left the church now except Karl, Kayleigh, Mike and Joanna.

"It's not that," said Karl. "I just don't want anyone getting involved in my problems. I don't want anyone else to get hurt."

Mike put a hand on Karl's right shoulder. "I understand that, Karl," he said, "but we want to help you if there is any trouble. Besides, Kayleigh also needs to get home safely. This way, both of you will be all right, and Joanna and I will both rest more easily tonight."

Mike looked at Joanna. She nodded in agreement.

Karl backed down: "I'm sorry," he replied. "I don't want any trouble to come to you because of me."

Mike shook his head. "Don't you go worrying about that! Now, let's get the two of you home."

The journey took only a couple of minutes. Karl was actually grateful for the ride. He thanked Mike and Joanna for the lift, and got out of the car with Kayleigh. As he did so, a police car could be heard approaching their side of the estate. Kayleigh also heard the siren and turned to look at Karl as Mike and Joanna departed.

"Sounds like trouble!" said Kayleigh.

"Yeah," said Karl thoughtfully; "I hope Richie isn't in it."

They said goodnight and went to their homes.

Unfortunately for Richie, he was on the estate as the police car approached. The Gang had called for Karl again and, having got no reply, they had made their way to the shops to buy some soft drinks and sweets. Having done so, they proceeded to Andrew's house. Andrew was just arriving back from visiting Tommy as the Gang turned up.

Williams boldly walked up to Andrew as he got out of the family car.

"Hey, Andy, we've been looking for you all night. Where 'ave you been?" he asked, ignoring Andrew's parents.

"I've been visiting Tommy," answered Andrew.

He was very unhappy that the Gang had turned up at his house.

"So, you coming out with us now?" Williams suggested.

"Come on, Andrew," said his dad. "Let's get inside. You can talk to your friends tomorrow at school."

"All right, mate! Keep yer 'air on! We only wanted to see Andy, that's all," said Williams.

"You lot can clear off!" ordered Andrew's dad. "It's because of you that my son is in hospital!"

Williams had taken it upon himself to be leader of the Gang in Jed's absence, and he began to curse and swear at Andrew's dad.

"We didn't do anything to Tommy, all right!" he argued.

"One more chance!" said Mr Young. "Clear off or I'll phone the police."

Andrew's dad ushered Andrew into the house. Williams picked up a stone and threw it at the living-room window. The impact cracked the pane. Andrew's mum screamed in the living room when she heard the glass crack, and Andrew's dad came running out of the house after the boys.

The Gang ran back towards the shopping centre.

Andrew's dad returned to the house and examined the damaged window.

"You shouldn't have done that!" cried Richie to Williams after the boys stopped running.

"Yeah? And who d'you think you are – my mother?" replied Williams.

He slapped Richie in the face.

"Ouch!" Richie shouted.

Williams ignored his cry of pain.

"You heard from Karl yet?" he asked, gesturing to Richie's mobile phone.

Richie checked his text messages.

"No – he hasn't replied."

"Well, text him again and see where he is. I'm not traipsing all over the estate looking for him."

Richie sent Karl another message.

When Karl received it, he decided to come up with an excuse to explain why he had been out. He didn't like lying to his friend, but he didn't want the Gang to turn up on his doorstep. He sent a message back to Richie informing him that he was at his grandmother's and wouldn't be home until much later.

When Richie received the message, he told Williams what Karl had said.

"Argh!" Williams went into a rage. "That Edwards is gonna pay! I've walked around this estate all night for nothing!"

In his anger, he snatched Richie's mobile phone out of his hand, ran towards the brook and threw it into the water.

"Hey!" cried Richie. "What did you do that for?"

"You wanna make something of it?" Williams challenged.

Suddenly another siren could be heard approaching the spot where the boys were.

"It's the cops!" cried Davison. "I'm getting out of 'ere!"

"Me too!" added Powell.

Before Richie knew what was happening, all the boys had dispersed, leaving him all alone to search the brook for his mobile phone.

CHAPTER SIXTEEN

That night, it seemed that chaos reigned on the estate. When Richie returned home and explained that his mobile phone was lost in the brook, his dad took him to Williams' house and demanded that the boy pay for a replacement. Although Williams protested his innocence, his dad didn't believe him. He apologised to both Richie and his dad and gave Richie some money to buy a new phone.

After Richie and his dad had left, Williams got a huge telling-off from his parents.

"You're grounded," said his mum, "until you pay your father back for that phone."

"But Mum!" protested Williams.

"No buts! You're grounded and that's final! You're not going out with the Gang again until it's paid for!"

Williams' younger brother spent the rest of the evening teasing him about being grounded. Williams now regretted what he had done to Richie's phone.

Throughout the night, more sirens could be heard across the estate. Outside the pub near the shopping centre, a fight had broken out. One of the men, who was partially drunk, fell into the road and was hit by a passing car. An ambulance had been dispatched to the scene as well as several police cars. The police had to deal with the man who had started the fight. After the accident he had taken his anger out on other people in the pub.

A short distance away from the shopping centre, obscured by a row of a garages, Jed and Cooper were drinking cans of lager and smoking, occasionally keeping an eye on the events outside the pub. Both boys were tired and hungry. It had been a busy night for them. After the incident with Richie and the Gang at the primary school, Jed, Cooper and Rogers had travelled across the city to another estate, where they had teamed up with a gang led by a friend of Jed's brother.

Jed wanted to settle a score with someone in another gang, and, when the two groups met, there was a huge fight. The police were called out to deal with the incident, and several arrests were made, but Jed, Cooper and Rogers got away from the scene using side streets and subways to get off the estate. Having caught a bus into the city centre again, they then proceeded by another bus to return to their own estate. Jed was satisfied that he had got even with his enemy.

Rogers had gone home, and Jed and Cooper had been heading for the chip shop in the shopping centre when the fight had occurred outside the pub. With the sound of the approaching police cars, the two boys had fled the area, keeping out of sight of the police, but still close enough to keep an eye on what was happening.

Cooper was keeping watch on the events at the bottom of the road as Jed finished his can of lager. He dropped the empty can to the floor and kicked it across the road.

"Looks like it's all over. The fuzz are leaving," declared Cooper.

"Good! We can get some chips," said Jed.

"What're you gonna say to your mum?"

"What about?"

"About your ol' man being arrested – about 'im starting the fight down there," said Cooper, pointing at the pub.

"Nothing. The fuzz'll probably tell her. Anyway, she's out tonight – won't be back 'til late."

"What about yer ol' man?" asked Cooper.

"Don't care!" answered Jed. "After what he did to me earlier, I hope 'e rots in jail!"

Jed's dad was the man who had started the fight. Jed had recognised him as they approached the shops before the sirens had begun, and he had seen his dad start the fight. He didn't care about the outcome – he had no feelings left for either of his parents.

The boys managed to buy something to eat just before the chip shop closed. Walking back home, Cooper chatted with Jed.

"What are we going to do tomorrow, Jed – go to school?"

"No chance! The fuzz will be there again – after tonight, we need to keep out of sight for a while. Rogers is gonna go. He's gonna let me know what happens with the Gang."

"What about Edwards and Young?" asked Cooper.

"I'll decide what to do with 'em after I 'ear from Rogers."

"Listen," said Cooper: "I've been thinking. What if Peters, Collins and Davison were telling the truth?"

Jed shrugged his shoulders. "What if they were? They got what they deserved for being disloyal to me."

"I don't mean that," replied Cooper. "If they were telling the truth, it means someone else grassed on you. It means someone else in the Gang is a traitor."

Jed thought for a moment.

"You mean we may have to do this all over again to one of the others?" he said.

"Well, if someone else has grassed, it means we can't trust 'em, don't it?"

"Yeah, mate," said Jed thoughtfully. "You could be right. We'll have to see if Rogers finds out anything tomorrow. He'll let us know if he does."

Jed and Cooper both finished their bags of chips, and threw

the chip papers disrespectfully into a garden they were passing as they walked home. They reached the street where they both lived. A police car was parked outside Jed's house and two officers were attempting to get a reply at his front door. Jed and Cooper doubled back and stayed out of sight until the two officers left the street.

"That was close!" admitted Cooper.

"Yeah," replied Jed, "it was."

The two boys agreed to meet each other the next day at a set time, and both went into their respective homes.

Jed's house was in complete darkness; there was no sign of life within its walls. He was all alone. His mum was still out, and he knew his dad would not be back after what had happened at the pub. The thought gave Jed an idea.

He made his way upstairs and entered his mum and dad's room. He crossed the room to his mum's dressing table, found her old jewellery box and lifted the lid. He pulled open one of the compartments and looked inside. Several £10 notes were rolled up and held together with an elastic band. It was his mum's bingo winnings. Jed took the money and counted it.

"Eighty quid!" he said greedily.

He pushed the money into a trouser pocket and closed the box carefully. He then went to his own room, opened the tin he kept under his bed and put the money inside it.

'When Mum finds out the money is missing, I'll deny taking it, and then she'll blame Dad,' he thought to himself. 'I can use the money quickly so she'll never find it.'

Jed closed his bedroom door and locked it. Then he opened his window, lay down on his bed and thought of the events of that evening. He felt very satisfied with himself, until Cooper's question came back to his mind: "What if Peters, Collins and Davison were telling the truth?" The thought angered him. He felt for the knife and the knuckleduster he kept in his jacket.

'I'm gonna 'ave to teach someone else a lesson about loyalty!' he thought to himself. Then he smiled as the pleasure of beating up another member of the Gang came into his mind.

CHAPTER SEVENTEEN

The following morning, Karl walked to school with Kayleigh, Debbie, David and Paul.

"I heard there was trouble at the pub last night," said David.

"Yeah," replied Debbie. "Dad said someone started a fight and got arrested. The bloke he fought got run over by a car."

As David and Debbie chatted about the details of the incident, Kayleigh turned to Karl.

"Did you hear any more from Richie last night?" she asked.

"Yeah. He sent me another text message. The Gang were still looking for me. I told him I was at my nan's. I didn't like lying to him, but it got me out of trouble for the night."

"Do you think Jed will be in school today?" asked Kayleigh.

"I doubt it. Rogers usually comes in, finds out everything Jed wants to know, then goes and tells him. I expect he'll have an excuse for not being in again."

Karl received some nasty looks from the Gang when he arrived at registration.

"Hey, Edwards," said Logan, "how's yer nan?"

"She's fine," replied Karl.

"Got back from there late, didn't you?" asked Powell sarcastically.

"Yeah, later than I planned. I had to do some chores for her."

Karl looked across at Kayleigh. She smiled and hoped that

the Gang would be convinced by his words.

"Jed wasn't pleased you didn't come out with us," said Peters. "He sent us all to find you and Andy."

"Why?" asked Karl. "Where did Jed go?"

Peters shrugged his shoulders. "I dunno. Said he had to take care of something."

Williams suddenly appeared at the door. He saw Richie, walked up to him and grabbed him by his shirt collar.

"Why, you little—"

"That's enough!" called Mrs Phillips. "Danny, let go of Richie, now!"

Williams pushed Richie back into his chair and went to his usual seat. As Mrs Phillips called the register, Karl wondered what the trouble was about. He decided to ask Richie when he got the opportunity.

Later that morning, Karl caught up with Andrew and Richie outside the school canteen, which was open for the students to buy fruit and other snacks at break time.

"All right, And?" asked Karl, queuing up behind him.

Andrew turned around.

"All right, Karl?" Andrew replied.

"How's Tommy doing?" asked Karl.

"He's getting better. He may be home this weekend."

The boys moved up to the till and paid for their snacks.

"That's good," replied Karl. "I'll call and see him when he comes home."

The Gang were already meeting together in their usual place. Williams was beginning to give out the orders, still thinking he was in charge without Jed around. Karl, Richie and Andrew avoided the area where the Gang were meeting and found another place on the school grounds to eat their snacks. There were several other groups of students standing nearby, and the boys found it difficult to find a quiet spot for themselves.

"So, what was all the trouble with Williams about this morning?" asked Karl.

"It's a long story," replied Richie.

As Karl finished his packet of crisps, Richie told them about the events of the night before: how Jed had turned up and taken the Gang to the old primary school; how he had left them to find Andrew and Karl; and how Williams had then thrown Richie's mobile phone into the brook.

"My dad went up his house and demanded that he pay for a new phone," explained Richie. "Williams' dad went spare. From what I've heard off the others, his mum has grounded him until he pays his old man back for the phone."

"I bet Williams won't like that!" exclaimed Andrew.

"Why was Jed looking for us last night?" asked Karl, taking a bite from his snack.

"He thought you had grassed on him," replied Richie. "Someone from the Gang told the cops about the incident at the flat. He thought it was one of us. Then he started on Collins, Davison and Peters. There was a huge punch-up between them."

"Well, I didn't say anything," said Karl.

"Neither did I," protested Richie, "so it must have been one of those three – although they said they didn't do it."

"I doubt if they would dare," said Karl. "They're too scared of Jed to turn him over to the cops."

"They didn't," said Andrew.

"How do you know?" asked Richie.

"Because I did," said Andrew solemnly.

"You did!" exclaimed Karl. "Why?"

"They interviewed me at lunchtime, before the rest of you," explained Andrew. "When the cops started asking all those questions, I just kept thinking of what Jed had done to Tommy. I decided to tell the truth. I felt it was the only way to see an end to all the trouble. I thought Jed would get caught if I confessed, but the police said they need more evidence. I didn't mean for anything to happen to anyone else. It's all my fault!"

"Don't blame yourself," said Karl. "You're not responsible for Jed's actions."

"I wish the cops could arrest Jed," said Andrew. "I hate him for what he did to my brother."

The bell rang for the end of break time. Karl, Richie and Andrew hurriedly finished their snacks and made their way to their next lesson, unaware that their conversation had been overheard. Rogers had followed the boys from the canteen and hidden himself behind another small crowd, close enough to hear everything they had said to one another. As the crowd of students moved towards their classrooms, Rogers grinned nastily.

'Jed is gonna love this when I tell 'im,' he said to himself.

Rogers made his way to his next lesson, making his plans to meet Jed later that day.

CHAPTER EIGHTEEN

As soon as the school bell rang for the end of the day, the boys from the Gang hurried out on to the estate, leaving behind them Karl, Richie and Andrew, who were making their way to the art room for the extra lesson organised by Mr Barnes.

Williams was facing an endless barrage of teasing from the other boys. They were not going to let him forget that he was grounded, and unable to come out with them that evening.

As the main body of the Gang made their way home, Rogers was making his own way to meet Jed and Cooper in their usual place on the rec. Cooper and Jed had spent the day with a friend of Jed's brother who had been a part of the gang which Jed had fought with the night before. Cooper nudged Jed as soon as Rogers came into sight.

"He's here, Jed!" said Cooper.

Jed finished a cigarette and stubbed it out.

"Well, Rogers," he asked sternly, "what's the score?"

Rogers began to relate everything that had happened that day. He told Jed firstly about Williams and his antics on the estate after the Gang had gone to call for Karl and Andrew.

"Apparently," Rogers continued, "the fool's gone and got himself grounded. His mum and dad won't let him out until he's paid for Richie's phone."

Jed looked at Cooper. Rogers carried on with his story.

"Logan said Williams was trying to run the Gang last night;

seems he thought he was in charge since you weren't around."

"Did he, now?" said Jed. "Cooper, we're definitely gonna have to do something about him. He's proving to be too big for his boots!"

Cooper nodded in agreement.

"So, what about Edwards and Young?"

"Well," answered Rogers, "Andy went to see Tommy with his mum and dad – that's for certain. As for Edwards, he says he went to his nan's, but I reckon he was out on the estate with that lot from the church. He seems to have become very friendly with Kayleigh, Debbie, David and Paul."

"I thought as much," said Jed. "I reckon he's the one that grassed on me!"

"No," said Rogers, "it was Andy. I heard him tell Richie and Karl at break time. It seems he was interviewed by the police yesterday lunchtime and told them everything because of what you did to Tommy. He hates you, Jed, and wants you locked up."

Jed's anger reached bursting point. He flew into a rage.

"I'm gonna get Young for this! What I did to Tommy is nothing compared to what I will do to 'im!"

Jed started to walk back to the estate.

"Where are you going, Jed?" asked Cooper.

"To Andy's house! I'm gonna get the little squealer!"

"He's not gone home yet," reported Rogers.

"Where is he, then?" asked Cooper.

"He stayed behind in school to do some artwork. So did Richie and Karl."

Jed laughed. "Perfect! I can get back at all three of them – and that blessed school at the same time. Come on – I know exactly what to do."

CHAPTER NINETEEN

The art room was a hive of activity. Several students from Karl's class were staying behind for the extra lesson to complete their project work. Richie and Debbie were working on computer design packages, while Kayleigh and two other students were completing some pottery work. Karl was busy using a charcoal pencil to put the finishing touches to a piece of work he had started a couple of weeks before.

Andrew and another student, Michaela, accompanied Mr Barnes to a stockroom where the Drama Department kept a large number of costumes for use in school productions. The stockroom was at the back of the school, one floor lower than the art room. It opened on to a corridor that ran the length of the building. At several points along the corridor stairways led to all the main areas of the school.

Andrew and Michaela were studying textiles, and Mr Barnes was showing them some different fabrics to give them ideas for their project work.

A number of teachers had already left before Jed, Cooper and Rogers began their assault on the school. Jed knew the layout of the school very well. He had broken into the building several times before. He knew where all the weak spots were, where he could get in easily, without detection.

Half an hour passed without any incident. All the students were getting on with their work, chatting amongst themselves and enjoying their time together. As Mr Barnes was finishing his lecture on textiles and costumes, one of the school cleaners suddenly knocked on the open door of the stockroom.

"Sorry to trouble you, sir," she said, "but I've seen some lad running up and down the corridor near the English Department. He's not one of your lot, is he?"

"I wouldn't think so," replied Mr Barnes. "Still, I'd better take a look, just in case." He turned back to Andrew and Michaela. "When you've finished, just shut the door and return to class. I'll lock the room up on my way back."

Mr Barnes headed towards the English Department, leaving Andrew and Michaela to continue their research.

Back in the art room, Kayleigh was putting the finishing touches to her piece of pottery. Karl wandered over to see how she was getting along.

"That looks good," he commented.

"Thanks. I've tried to get this right several times. I think I've got it now."

Richie got up from the computer to stretch his legs, and he also took a look at Kayleigh's work.

"What are you doing after school, Karl?" he asked.

"I dunno. I haven't got any plans," replied Karl.

"How about coming over to my house? You can have a go at my new football game on the computer."

"Is football all you two think about?" asked Kayleigh.

Karl and Richie looked at each other and smiled.

"Yeah, pretty much," replied Karl.

Kayleigh shook her head in disbelief, and returned her concentration to her piece of pottery.

Mr Barnes saw someone running about the school, but the boy was so far away from him that he was unable to catch him. The teacher went to the school office and reported the incident to the school secretary. The headmaster, who was talking to two other teachers, overheard Mr Barnes and asked him to explain what was happening.

Michaela yawned as she put her final notes down in her workbook.

"Well, that's me done," she said cheerfully. "I'm going back to class. You coming, Andy?"

"You go on. I'm almost finished," Andrew replied.

"OK. See you in a few minutes."

Michaela closed her workbook and made her way back to the art room, leaving Andrew alone in the stockroom.

The students in the art room were coming towards the completion of their work when Michaela walked in. Several heads turned towards her as she entered the room.

"Hey, Micky, where's Andy?" asked Richie.

"He hasn't finished yet – said he'd be along in a moment," Michaela replied.

"Where's Mr Barnes?" asked Debbie. "We haven't seen him all lesson."

"Oh, one of the cleaners told him she had seen someone running about the school, so he went to investigate it."

"Sounds odd!" said Debbie. "I hope he gets back soon. I've finished what I need to do; I want to go home."

Andrew was just putting things away when he heard a noise outside the stockroom.

"I've nearly finished, sir," he said, thinking it was Mr Barnes.

"Have you?"

Andrew froze at the sound of a familiar voice. Slowly, he turned around. Standing outside the door were Jed and Cooper.

"Well, well! Takin' up your time with clothes now, eh? I always said there was something odd about you," remarked Jed.

Cooper laughed.

"W-what are you two doing here?" Andrew asked nervously.

"Well, it's like this, see?" said Jed. "A little voice told me you've been squealing to the fuzz, so I need to find out for myself whether you have or not."

"How did you know where I was?" asked Andrew.

Jed laughed. "Easy! We came round the back way into the school, just as you an' Micky were arriving with Barnesy."

"Well, I have to get back to class," said Andrew, making a move for the door.

Jed stepped forward, blocking the doorway to prevent Andrew escaping his clutches.

"I don't think so!" he said sternly.

"Come on, Jed! Mr Barnes will be back any minute. You won't get away with anything."

Jed laughed again. "Barnesy won't be able to help you! Rogers is giving him the run-around. And neither will your friends be able to get you out of this one! OK, Cooper, do it!"

Jed punched Andrew several times in the stomach, causing him to fall backwards into the clothes rack at the back of the room. Cooper then lit a match.

"Hey! What are you doing?" gasped Andrew, trying to regain his footing.

"What d'you think we're doing?" laughed Cooper.

Cooper held the lit match to the corner of a cardboard box that lay on the floor. It contained old costumes that had been used in previous stage productions.

"No! Don't!" pleaded Andrew.

He tried to push Cooper away, but Jed pinned him to the back wall of the stockroom. Cooper lit several more matches and held them to the cardboard box. Moments later the flames caught some old curtains and smoke began to rise out of the room. Jed hit Andrew again and he fell to the floor.

"That'll teach you for grassin' on me!" yelled Jed.

Jed and Cooper closed the door, shutting Andrew inside.

"Job done! Let's go!" ordered Jed.

The two boys ran to the nearest stairway and quickly made their way outside. They ran across the school field towards the hedgerow that separated the school from a farm, leaving Andrew to recover from his encounter with Jed and fight his way out of the smoke-filled room!

CHAPTER TWENTY

Andrew had been right about one thing: Mr Barnes was returning. He saw Jed and Cooper from the far end of the corridor.

"Hey!" he bellowed. "What do you think you're doing?"

Jed and Cooper were out of sight when Mr Barnes arrived at the storeroom moments later and saw smoke coming from under the door. He heard a thumping noise coming from inside the room. As he opened the door, Andrew fell out of the room and Mr Barnes caught him before he hit the floor.

Andrew was coughing loudly, having inhaled some of the smoke. Mr Barnes supported him and led him into the open air. As they passed a fire alarm on the corridor wall, Mr Barnes smashed it with his right elbow, and the fire bell sounded all around the school.

In the art room, most of the students had finished their work when they heard the fire bell ring.

"What's that?" asked Michaela.

"It's the fire bell, silly," said Debbie.

"Well, what's it ringing for?" asked Michaela.

Debbie shrugged her shoulders. "I dunno. It's probably being tested to make sure it works properly."

No one in the room expected there to be any danger, and the class continued to wait for Mr Barnes to return, unaware that the storeroom was on fire. Running footsteps could soon be heard outside the Art Department, and, moments later, the cleaner who had spoken to Mr Barnes earlier entered the room in a hurry.

"Quickly!" she ordered. "There's a fire on the lower level. You must all leave the building via the nearest fire exit!"

Michaela gasped. "Andrew is still on the lower level!"

Debbie turned around and looked out of the window at the front of the classroom.

"No he's not – look!" she cried, pointing out of the window.

Mr Barnes had helped Andrew around the side of the school and was now standing in the car park, helping Andrew breathe more easily.

The art class left via the nearest fire exit, and moments later they were also standing in the car park. The staff who had remained at the school, including the headmaster, had now joined the pupils and Mr Barnes. Mr Barnes told the Headmaster what he had seen, and where the seat of the fire was.

A few minutes later, the Fire Brigade arrived on the scene and began to get the situation under control. A police car also turned up, and the headmaster gave the police the details Mr Barnes had told him. A paramedic arrived shortly after, and he checked Andrew over to make sure he was all right.

When Kayleigh saw the paramedic attending to Andrew, she tapped Debbie on the shoulder and called her over to where she was standing with Karl.

"Quickly, let's pray that Andrew will be all right," she suggested.

The rest of the class were too busy watching the events unfold in front of them to pay any attention to the three prayer warriors. Holding hands, Kayleigh led them in a short prayer and asked the Lord to protect Andrew from serious injury. As soon as the prayer was finished, Kayleigh had a deep sense of peace. She knew the Lord was looking after their injured friend. Their prayer had been answered.

Moments later, the paramedic confirmed that Andrew was well enough to go home, thanks to the quick reactions of Mr Barnes.

The firemen had the blaze under control very quickly, and before long the building was being ventilated to clear the remaining smoke from the classrooms. The damage from the fire was not as bad as the firemen had expected, although the storeroom and all its contents had been completely destroyed.

The headmaster telephoned Andrew's mum, explained the situation, and asked her to pick Andrew up from school. While they waited for Andrew's mum to arrive, Andrew told Karl what had happened.

"They came from nowhere. Jed punched me to the ground and Cooper set the room on fire!"

"Are you sure it was Cooper, not Jed?" asked Karl.

"Yeah, Jed was holding me against the wall so I couldn't stop Cooper setting fire to the box of costumes."

The headmaster was standing nearby, listening to their conversation. When Andrew's mum arrived, he told her what had happened. While the paramedic was giving her advice on looking after Andrew, the headmaster turned to the art students.

"You can all go home now. I expect your parents will be wondering where you are."

"Sir, will the school be open tomorrow?" asked Debbie.

"I will have to check with the Fire Brigade, but I should think so," he replied.

Some of the students moaned at the news. After all that had happened that evening, they were hoping for a day off. The class began to walk home, leaving Andrew and his mum to speak to the police.

"What were you talking to Andrew about, Karl?" asked Debbie nosily.

"Andy said that Jed and Cooper started the fire," answered Karl.

"What! They couldn't have!" exclaimed Richie. "They weren't even in school today. How did they know we were all staying behind?"

There was a pause. Karl shrugged his shoulders.

He was about to say that he didn't know, when he saw someone he recognised running across the playing field towards the perimeter fence.

"Rogers!" he said firmly, pointing to the figure in the distance.

"Yeah, it certainly looks like him," said Michaela.

"He was in school this morning! I bet he went to see Jed after school and told him what we were all doing!"

"Yeah," said Michaela. "One of the cleaners said she saw someone running around the corridors. Perhaps it was him!"

"To distract Mr Barnes," said Debbie.

"So Jed and Cooper could find Andy and start the fire," suggested Richie.

"It certainly fits," said Kayleigh thoughtfully.

"If it's true, the police need to be told," said Debbie.

"Yeah," said Karl, "but that's not all they need to know."

"What do you mean by that?" asked Debbie. "Do you know something we don't?"

Karl looked at Richie. Richie shook his head. He didn't want Karl to say any more, but Karl knew it was time to own up.

"Yeah, we know plenty," admitted Karl, "and the sooner the cops know it too, the better."

"Don't, Karl!" warned Richie. "If Jed finds out, he'll—"

"I have to take that chance," replied Karl. "It's time Jed was punished for his actions!"

Karl turned to face Kayleigh. "I'll call for you later," he said, smiling.

"Do you want me to come with you?" asked Kayleigh.

"No. This is something I have to do alone."

Kayleigh nodded solemnly. "OK, Karl. Be careful."

Karl looked at her and nodded, as if to agree he would be.

Leaving Richie and the girls behind him, Karl made his way home hastily in order to phone the police.

CHAPTER TWENTY-ONE

When Karl arrived home, he ran upstairs to his bedroom and found the card PC Hall had given him when he was interviewed at the school. As he got changed, he thought about what he would say to the police. He became very nervous, and hesitated.

Karl went downstairs and warmed his tea up in the microwave oven. As he ate it, he thought of Kayleigh and all she had been through with her great-grandmother. He regained his courage, finished his tea, rang the number and asked to speak to PC Hall. He was put through to her office, and a few moments later she received Karl's call.

"Hello, this is PC Hall. Can I help you?"

"Hello. PC Hall, this is Karl Edwards, from the high school."

"Oh yes. Hello, Karl. Are you all right after the events of tonight?"

"Yes, I'm fine, thanks." Karl hesitated.

"Did you want to speak to me about something, Karl?" asked PC Hall encouragingly.

Karl regained his nerve. "Uh, yeah, I did actually."

Karl told PC Hall that he had seen Rogers running away from the school before he left with his friends. PC Hall made some notes as Karl spoke, and she began to plan a visit to see Rogers at his home.

"Thank you for your information, Karl. That's very helpful."

"Wait!" said Karl. "There is something else – about Jed."

Karl hesitated again. This time the silence was longer.

"Karl? Hello, Karl. Are you still there?"

"Uh, yeah, I am."

"You wanted to say something about Jed?" asked PC Hall.

"Uh, yeah."

PC Hall sensed that Karl was feeling very nervous.

"Would you like to come to the station and talk, rather than discuss this over the phone?" she asked.

"Well, I would – I mean, I am willing to, but I'm concerned the Gang will be out looking for me," said Karl honestly.

"I see. Have you been having more trouble with them?"

"Well, no, not really, but after what happened to Andrew tonight I don't want to take any risks, if you know what I mean."

"I understand," said PC Hall. "OK, then, how about if Sergeant Haynes and myself call to see you in, say, about half an hour? Perhaps you would feel more comfortable talking to us at home."

"Yeah, that would be great!" said Karl.

"OK, we'll see you in half an hour, then. Goodbye, Karl."

"Goodbye."

Karl put the phone down. He felt relieved that the conversation was over. Then he tensed up again. He looked through the living-room window to see if anyone from the Gang was about, then he picked up his keys, mobile phone and denim jacket and headed for the front door. He wanted to do something before the police arrived that was just as important in his eyes as talking to them.

Kayleigh sat in tears as Karl admitted to her and her parents that he had known it was Jed and the Gang who had vandalised her great-grandmother's flat and caused her injuries.

"I'm going to be speaking to the police in a few minutes," he said, "and I wanted you to know before I told them the truth. I – I'm sorry I didn't say anything before. I was so scared of Jed that I bottled it in the interview. I am very sorry to you all."

Kayleigh's dad smiled at Karl and said, "I think we can all understand the predicament you were in, Karl. Be assured, none of us blame you personally for what happened. It took a lot of guts to come and tell us, and that shows a lot about you as a person. You will always be welcome here, any time."

Karl noticed the clock on the wall of the living room, and he stood up to go. "I have to get back for the police," he said.

Kayleigh left the room in tears, and ran upstairs. Karl looked concernedly at her mum and dad.

"Will Kayleigh be all right?" he asked. "I didn't mean to upset any of you."

"I'm sure she'll be fine," said her dad comfortingly.

Kayleigh's mum surprised Karl by giving him a hug.

"You take care of yourself. If you need anything, we are always here. God bless, Karl."

Karl said goodbye, and Kayleigh suddenly descended the stairs, wearing her denim jacket.

"I'll walk back to the house with you," she said.

"Oh, OK, then," said Karl, surprised at her decision.

Kayleigh turned to her mum. "Mum, I'm going to pop up to Deb's for a few minutes."

"OK, love," her mum replied.

It didn't take long to return to his house, and in that time Kayleigh and Karl said nothing at all. Karl suspected she was going to tell him she never wanted to see him again.

Turning to go into the house, Karl looked back at her and said, "Kayleigh, I'm sorry I upset you tonight. I should have told you the truth before."

Kayleigh shook her head. "You didn't upset me, Karl," she replied.

"Then why were you crying?"

"Because you've changed so much in the last couple of weeks. I felt so proud of you when you spoke to my parents tonight."

"Oh!" said Karl.

Kayleigh kissed him on the cheek.

"Why don't you call for me again after the police have gone? I won't be long at Debbie's."

Karl felt surprised at her invitation.

"Yeah, I'll do that," he said, smiling gently at her.

"I'll see you in about an hour."

"OK, then," said Karl.

The two friends parted company, and Karl entered the house. He took his jacket off and entered the living room. He checked the time: five minutes to go before the police were due to arrive. Karl suddenly felt nervous. What if he bottled it again? What if he was charged along with the Gang for the trouble on the estate? What if his evidence was not enough for the police to arrest Jed?

He sat down and took a deep breath. Then he remembered how Kayleigh had prayed at the school earlier, and he looked up to the ceiling in the hope that he could pray the right words.

"Lord, I'm going to tell the police what I know about the trouble the Gang has caused on the estate. Please help me to tell the truth. I want my life to change, and I want the trouble to stop." He could think of nothing else to add, so he sat in silence for a few moments. Then, as he said "Amen", the doorbell rang.

CHAPTER TWENTY-TWO

Karl opened the front door expecting to see the two police officers standing in front of him; but he was wrong. Jed stood on the doorstep, and the rest of the Gang stood in a huddled group behind him.

"Hello, Edwards. Long time, no see!"

Karl composed himself.

"What do you want, Jed?"

"What d'you think? We normally meet up at this time of night, don't we?"

Karl decided to stand his ground.

"I can't tonight, Jed. I'm seeing someone in a short while."

"Oh yeah, your new girlfriend? I've heard all about you two lovebirds."

Some of the boys laughed and Rogers gave a wolf whistle. Karl was glad of the distraction from the subject of the police, and he played along with it.

"Yeah, I'm seeing Kayleigh later. So what?"

Jed turned and gestured to Rogers and Cooper. They had been obscured from Karl's view by the rest of the Gang. The boys passed through the small crowd, dragging Richie between them. Karl almost had to look away. Richie had been beaten up by Jed, and his face was badly bruised and bleeding.

"What happened to you?" Karl asked.

"He fell off his bike – what do you think?" remarked Rogers.

Cooper laughed.

Karl felt himself tense up. His anger began to build towards Jed.

"Now," said Jed, "either you come out with us, or I'll finish Richie off for good!"

Karl was very concerned for his friend. He decided to back down and hope the police would turn up before any trouble took place.

"I'll get my jacket," he said, and went into the house.

As he picked it up, he said a quick prayer: "Lord, help me please! And Richie! Please get us out of this mess."

"Edwards! Come on!" Jed bellowed through the open door.

Karl emerged wearing his jacket and closed the door behind him. Rogers and Cooper walked behind Karl as if they were escorting him somewhere. Karl knew there was going to be trouble and that he had to keep the Gang in the street until the police turned up. He kept praying in his mind, asking the Lord to help him out of the predicament. As they passed Kayleigh's house, Karl came up with an idea. He bent down and fiddled with his laces, pretending they had come undone.

"Come on, Edwards – I haven't got all night!" bellowed Jed.

Kayleigh's mum and dad heard Karl's name being shouted in the street. They went to the window and discreetly looked outside.

"It's Jed!" said Kayleigh's dad.

"I'll phone the police," said Kayleigh's mum. "It looks like there's going to be some trouble with that lot."

Karl stood up and said to Jed, "Where are we going anyway?"

"The usual place. Where d'you think?" replied Jed.

"I'm not sure Richie is up to walking that far," said Karl, trying to delay Jed further.

Jed turned round.

"I don't care what you think, Edwards! Come on, or else I'll do you over just like 'im!"

"Why did you do Richie over, anyway?" asked Karl bravely.

Jed walked up to Karl and confronted him.

"Cos I've had more fuzz at my house tonight! Seems there was a fire at the school and it's being blamed on me! Richie here told the fuzz I started it – unless it was you!"

Karl knew the only way to stop Jed leaving the street was to do something to get him riled. As Jed walked back to the front of the group, Karl decided to throw him a bluff.

"Yeah, I did actually," he said calmly.

It worked. Jed flew into a rage.

"You did what!"

Jed marched back to Karl, grabbed him by the collar of his jacket, and pulled Karl to his face.

"Well, it was the least I could do after you tried to get Andy framed for it!"

Rogers, Cooper and Jed looked at one another as Jed released his grip on Karl.

"What are you talking about, Edwards?" asked Cooper.

"When he was rescued from the fire, Andy told me what you guys did. He told me you lot started it!"

"That's rubbish! We weren't anywhere near the school!" denied Rogers.

Karl turned away from Jed and confronted Rogers.

"Yes, you were. I saw you running across the playing field."

Karl saw the anger in Rogers' face. He knew what was coming, but all he could do, if he wanted to delay the Gang any further, was to stand there and take it.

Rogers snapped. "You little grass! I'll make you pay for this!"

He punched Karl in the stomach and face and he fell to the ground. As Karl lay on the pavement, Rogers began to kick him repeatedly in his stomach and chest.

Kayleigh's parents saw it all. Kayleigh's mum, who was on the phone to the police, reported what was happening. Kayleigh's dad had run upstairs to the main bedroom and, using his camcorder, he filmed everything the boys were doing in the street.

Rogers pinned Karl to the ground and continually punched him. Karl tried to wrestle his way out of Rogers' grip, but it was no use. As the boys looked on, Karl grew weaker and weaker with every punch, until there seemed to be no fight left in him. Rogers finally got up and turned to Jed.

"Do you want a piece of 'im, or shall I finish 'im off?"

"In a minute," said Jed, turning to Richie. "Well, it seems like you didn't grass on me after all. So what do you know about Andy's story?"

Richie coughed and spoke wearily. "I didn't speak to Andy at school. Only Karl did. I only know what Karl told you."

"And did you see Rogers leaving the school as well?" Jed asked, taking hold of his knuckleduster inside his jacket.

"Yeah, we all saw him," admitted Richie.

"Who's *we*?" asked Jed sternly.

Richie thought for a moment.

"There was Karl, Michaela, Kayleigh, Debbie and me. We walked home together."

Jed was enraged! He removed the knuckleduster from his pocket and turned, to everyone's surprise, to Rogers. He punched him hard in the stomach, and Rogers cried out in agony.

"How could you have been so stupid – letting that lot see you leaving the school! Idiot!"

"I didn't know, Jed, I swear!" pleaded Rogers, holding an arm out to fend Jed off.

Jed took out his knife, grabbed Rogers by the collar, and pulled him up against the garden wall outside Kayleigh's house.

"Don't you ever let me down again – got it?"

He pressed the blade of the knife against Rogers' left cheek.

"I won't, Jed – honest! I'm sorry!"

Karl had never seen Rogers so fearful of Jed, nor Jed so enraged by one of his best friends. Jed turned back to face the rest of the Gang.

"And that goes for you lot, an' all! Anyone else lets me down and I'll kill yer! Now come on!"

The other boys just looked on fearfully, not knowing what to say or do. Williams gestured to the others, and they began to follow Jed.

As Karl got to his feet, Jed pulled Cooper away from the rest of the group and spoke to him alone. Karl struggled over to Richie to see how he was.

"Are you OK?" he asked, knowing Richie wasn't.

"I feel terrible," said Richie. "I just wanna go home."

Karl nodded gently. He began to pray again for the Lord to show him a way out for the two of them. Another idea entered his mind.

"Just do what I say," said Karl quietly, and he whispered something to Richie.

Cooper and Jed walked back to the Gang, and Cooper spoke to the boys.

"Come on, you lot! Let's get to the rec, now!"

As they all began to make their way out of the street, Richie suddenly groaned, appeared to faint, and fell to the floor. Karl quickly examined Richie.

"Richie can't make it," said Karl, leaning over his friend. "He's too weak!"

Jed couldn't accept Karl's words. He marched up to Richie, pulled him up by the collar and held the knife to his throat.

"You'd better come with us now, or I'll finish you off for good!"

"He's too weak, Jed! He needs to go home," stated Karl.

Jed let go of Richie, who slumped to the floor, and he confronted Karl again.

"I've had it with you two! You're always causing me trouble! You'd better get your pal on his feet or I'll finish you off an' all!"

"Try it!" shouted a female voice.

Jed, still holding the knife out in a threat to Karl, suddenly felt the blade being kicked out of his hand. Turning in surprise to his left side, he couldn't believe his eyes.

"I'll get you for that!" he shouted.

He charged towards the female, who was standing in a defensive posture she had learned in a martial-arts class. Jed lunged at her, but she simply stepped aside and cracked Jed on the back of the neck with her right hand as he passed her. Jed went flying, tripped on the kerb and fell head first into the side of a wheelie bin.

"You want some more? Bring it on, tough guy!" challenged Debbie.

None of the boys could believe what they were seeing. The toughest bully in the school was being beaten by a girl!

Jed got to his feet.

"You little—"

He was still wearing his knuckleduster, and he threw himself forward again to attack Debbie. Debbie again stepped to one side, grabbed Jed's leading arm, twisted it behind his back and kicked him in the stomach. Jed again fell to the ground, and Debbie took up another defensive pose.

Debbie sniggered. "Ha! You ain't so tough after all!"

The rest of the boys were so shocked by what was happening that they did not notice the police cars approaching them from the far end of the street until it was too late.

Peters looked up and suddenly shouted, "It's the fuzz! Run for it!"

The boys turned and ran past Kayleigh's house, only to find the other end of the street blocked by two police vans. There were police officers everywhere, some with dogs. Although the boys tried desperately to get away, the police rounded up the majority of them in a matter of moments. Jed had just risen to his feet when two officers wrestled him to the ground and arrested him.

Cooper had noticed where Jed's knife had landed. He jumped over Kayleigh's garden wall on to the lawn where it lay, and picked it up. His mind was spinning. Without thinking about his actions, he charged at Debbie with the knife held in front of him, screaming at the top of his voice.

"Debbie!" shrieked Kayleigh, who was standing some distance away from the fight.

Karl heard Kayleigh's cry, looked up and saw the danger. He charged at Cooper, and wrestled him to the ground before he could reach Debbie with the knife. Cooper was a lot stronger than Karl, though, and easily overcame him. As Karl lay on the floor, weak and unable to defend himself, Cooper thrust the knife at him.

"Argh!"

The cry of pain could be heard all along the street.

CHAPTER TWENTY-THREE

Karl felt something brush past his left side, and Cooper was pulled away. Looking up, he saw Cooper lying on his back, with one of the police dogs standing over him. The dog had charged at Cooper on the command of its handler, lunged at him and dragged him away from Karl. The dog pinned Cooper down until two police officers moved in to arrest him. Then the dog was restrained by its handler.

Cooper cursed and swore as he struggled with the two police officers on his way to the waiting police van. Jed was led away at the same time. As Karl got up from the ground, Jed spat and swore at him.

"You grass! I hate you, Edwards! Just you wait! I'll get even with you, I swear!"

"That's enough!" ordered one of the policemen. "Get a move on!"

Karl sighed deeply as he watched Jed enter the back of one of the police vans. He felt the left side of his face. It was sore from where he had taken blows from Rogers and Cooper.

Then he remembered Richie! He walked over to where Richie was lying and leaned over him. Richie was being attended to by PC Hall, Debbie, Kayleigh and Kayleigh's parents. When Kayleigh saw Karl, she threw her arms around him and hugged him.

"Oh, Karl! When I saw Cooper with that knife I – I thought you were done for!"

"So did I," admitted Karl. "Thank God for that police dog!" Karl turned to Debbie. "Thanks for your help, Debs."

"You too," replied Debbie.

"I didn't know you could do all that stuff."

"I go to a class each week," she confessed. "I never thought I'd use it against Jed, though."

Karl leaned over Richie.

"Is he going to be OK?" he asked PC Hall, who was kneeling at Richie's side.

"I hope so," the officer replied. "I've called for an ambulance. He's going to need medical attention."

She looked over her shoulder at Karl, and stood up next to him.

"So do you, by the look of things," she said, examining the side of Karl's face.

"Oh, I'm OK – just a few bruises, that's all."

"You look pretty badly hurt from where I'm standing. You're to go to hospital too. That's an order!"

"But—"

"No buts! You've got a nasty graze on the left side of your face, Karl, and your left eye is swollen. Like it or not, you need those injuries seen to."

Reluctantly, Karl agreed. When the ambulance arrived, he joined Richie for the journey to the hospital.

"I'll see you soon," he said to Kayleigh as he boarded the ambulance.

"I'll be praying for you," replied Kayleigh.

The ambulance left, and PC Hall and Sergeant Haynes finished with their inquiries. Then they visited Richie's parents to inform them of what had happened. They also visited Karl's grandparents. Karl's grandfather rang Karl's mum at work and told her the news. After the police had left, he picked her up and took her to the hospital.

Richie slipped in and out of consciousness a couple of times in the ambulance. On arriving at the hospital, he was given immediate attention, as was Karl. Karl was treated for his injuries and sent for a series of X-rays to make sure no bones were broken. By now, Karl was beginning to feel weak and dizzy and, on returning to the Accident and Emergency ward, he was sick. The doctor decided to keep him in overnight for observation, so his mum stayed with him to make sure he was all right.

Richie's parents also stayed the night, waiting for news of their son, who was undergoing surgery for his facial injuries.

In the afternoon of the following day, Karl was discharged from hospital with a sick note for his school. He was told to go home and rest, and return to the hospital for a check-up in a week's time. Karl's face was very sore, especially around his left eye, but compared to Richie he knew he had got off lightly.

Richie was put under close observation on one of the wards after his operation. No one knew how long he would have to stay in the hospital.

The following day, Karl was visited by PC Hall and Sergeant Haynes. They talked about the incident in the street as well as what would be happening to members of the Gang. Sergeant Haynes informed Karl and his mum that Jed and Cooper were being held at a Young Offenders' Centre until their case came up in court.

"They won't be coming back to the estate for a long time," explained the Sergeant, "and even when they do there will be restrictions on where they can go. Their movements will be limited."

"What about the rest of the Gang?" asked Karl's mum.

"We'll be keeping a close eye on all of them. If any of them step out of line, they'll be in big trouble!"

Karl turned to PC Hall.

"I was going to tell you the other night that it was Jed that caused the damage to Mrs Evans' flat."

"I thought it was going to be something like that," replied PC Hall. "We spoke to Tommy on Monday. He told us the same thing."

"Oh," said Karl, a little disappointed that he wasn't the one to break the news.

"But your evidence will still help us," said Sergeant Haynes. "Perhaps, when you feel better, you could give us a statement about Jed and Cooper's activities on the estate."

"Yeah, I'll do that," agreed Karl, fearlessly.

The two officers got up to leave, and Karl thanked them both for all their help. PC Hall turned to him.

"You've nothing to fear any more, Karl. The trouble with the Gang is over," she said, smiling.

Karl saw them to the door, and then went for a rest. As he lay on his bed, he thought of PC Hall's words:

"You've nothing to fear any more, Karl. The trouble with the Gang is over."

Karl looked at the ceiling.

"Thank you, God," he said quietly.

Then he closed his eyes and drifted into a peaceful, dreamless sleep.

CHAPTER TWENTY-FOUR

By the weekend, Karl was beginning to feel better. On Saturday evening, Kayleigh, Debbie, Michaela, David and Paul visited him. The group spent the time watching one of the music channels on television and talking about the events of the week, including what had been happening in school since Jed and Cooper had been arrested.

"All the boys in our year are scared stiff of Debbie now!" said Paul.

"Yeah," said Michaela, "after they heard what Debs did to Jed, they won't go anywhere near her!"

Karl smiled. "I'm not surprised! You should have seen her tackle Jed! The look of shock on his face!"

"I wish I'd seen it," said David.

"Well, it was about time Jed was put in his place," said Debbie.

The evening passed quickly. When it was time for his friends to go home, Karl thanked them for visiting him. David, Paul and Debbie agreed to walk Michaela back to her house, and they went on their way, leaving Kayleigh and Karl alone.

As Kayleigh put her jacket on, Karl said, "I'm sorry for all the trouble the Gang caused the other night. Please thank your parents for all their help for me."

"I will," replied Kayleigh, checking her mobile phone.

"You know," Karl continued, "when Jed turned up and I saw the state Richie was in, I did a lot of praying. And – you know what? – it really did work!"

"I told you it would," said Kayleigh, smiling.

"I've been thinking over the last few days," said Karl. "I don't really understand all that much about faith and what you believe at the church, but I was wondering whether you could help me figure it all out sometime?"

"Of course," said Kayleigh cheerfully. "How about tomorrow night? You can take me out and we can talk about it then."

"Take you out?" asked Karl, puzzled. "Where to?"

"To church, silly! We can go to the service and then have a discussion in the 'After Church' meeting."

Karl laughed. "Oh, yeah, I'd forgotten it's church tomorrow."

Kayleigh looked at Karl.

"Well, I have to go. You take it easy and I'll see you tomorrow."

She gave Karl a hug.

As they stood at the door, Karl said, "You know, I owe you a great deal of thanks for all you've done for me."

"Oh, it was nothing really."

"No, Kayleigh, it really was. I wouldn't be out of the Gang and all that trouble without your help and support. Thanks. I really mean it! Thanks."

Kayleigh felt slightly embarrassed.

"I've been praying for you for a long time, Karl. Somebody told me to back last year."

"Oh? Who was that?" asked Karl curiously.

Kayleigh pointed and looked upwards. "The Lord," she said. "He's the One you should thank, not me."

When Karl returned to the living room, he thought about what Kayleigh had said to him on the doorstep. Then he thought about all the things he had done with the Gang. He realised that she was telling the truth, and he said, "Thank you, Lord, for everything."

A sense of peace came over Karl as he sat back on the settee. He somehow knew that a new life of faith and a better way of living was about to begin.